MENAGERIE 3

MENAGERIE 3

Indonesian Fiction • Poetry • Photographs • Essays

John H. McGlynn, Series Editor

LONTAR

The Lontar Foundation, Jakarta

Manufactured in Indonesia.

Design : Jessy Tansil & John H. McGlynn
Layout : Burke Broholm & Bless Lexy Soeitoe
Cover artwork : *Buruh Perempuan di antara Pabrik dan Penjara (Woman Workers between the Factory and Prison),* detail of a painting by Semsar Siahaan, from the collection of Hariman Siregar; oil on canvas, 1 x 1 m.; 1992
Cover photograph : Mohamad Firman Ichsan
Typeface : Palatino, Helvetica Narrow
Printer : PT. Sembrani Aksara Nusantara

ISBN No. 979-8083-23-7

Editor's Note

THE LONTAR FOUNDATION'S WORK is made possible, in large part, through assistance from Friends of Lontar, a group of concerned corporations, institutions, and individuals who share Lontar's goal of promoting knowledge of Indonesian literary and artistic traditions. From the publication of books such as *Menagerie 3* to the production of films on Indonesian writers, it is Lontar's friends who make our work possible.

The names of individuals who support Lontar's work are too numerous to list here. However, Lontar would like to express its sincere thanks to the institutions and corporations who have contributed significantly to Lontar's activities fund during the past year. They include Rajawali Corporation, PT Kodel, Matra Magazine, PT Danamon, The Regent-Jakarta, Kresna Group, PT Freeport Indonesia, PT Excelcomindo, PT Ericsson, The Grand Hyatt, Garuda Indonesia Airways and The Ford Foundation.

On a more person level, as Lontar's editor-in-chief, I would like to express my thanks to the Idrus estate for its permission to publish the short stories by Idrus that appear herein and to reprint photographs from Mrs. Idrus' personal collection. I would also like to express my thanks to Margot Cohen and Karin Johnson for their editorial assistance.

John H. McGlynn

Contents

MENAGERIE 3

MARTYN COVE

Idrus: 1921-1979

IDRUS, ONE OF INDONESIA'S BEST KNOWN WRITERS and story-tellers, is often regarded as the satirist of his literary generation. He mapped out new directions for the use of the Indonesian language, strengthening it with a measure of frankness and directness that was uncommon before his time. He rose to prominence during the Indonesian revolution and has remained a respected literary figure ever since.

Idrus was born September 22, 1921 in Padang, West Sumatra, and spent his early years there. His father died when he was seven, and he and his mother and sister went to live with his father's parents. His grandfather was a merchant who traded in rattan, used for basketry and wickerwork. Unfortunately, the rattan market in Padang collapsed under pressure from Dutch colonial interests and times became more difficult. After his grandfather died, Idrus was brought up by his mother and her parents.

Reportedly, Idrus was not an easy child to handle, already showing a strong independent streak at a very young age. As a young boy he attended the mosque regularly and studied the Koran. Like other boys, once he had completed a successful reading of the entire Arabic text his family honored him with a special celebration. He then went on to read the Koran again, and again, and was rewarded twice more. Then a problem arose:

Idrus had a pet dog that was his constant companion. Dogs have an equivocal position in any Muslim society and are regarded as unclean, but young Idrus could see no reason why his pet should not be allowed to accompany him to the mosque, and when the religious authorities objected to his dog's presence, he refused to attend. The family was mortified but Idrus could not be moved, in spite of his youth. And so ended Idrus' formal religious life.

THE SMILING HAWAIAN PLAYERS - Padang, West Sumatra 1937
Idrus sitting, fourth from right

Idrus attended the local Dutch colonial secondary school. He was bright, but rather more interested in music than in study. As a young teenager he played the guitar and set up a band with some friends. It was called — typically for the thirties — The Smiling Hawaiian Players. The group played regularly at the Padang Club, the social center for Padang's expatriate community. In their tropical whites, the local Dutch businessmen and planters — some of whom no doubt had helped to rob his grandfather of his business — lounged around the verandah and the bar, drinking schnapps and beer in the warm tropical evenings while young Idrus and his friends, decked out in Hawaiian shirts, strummed hulas and dance tunes.

This was more fun than school and Idrus neglected his studies. By the time he was seventeen and going into his fourth year of high school, it was clear that something would have to be done to get him back on track. The year was 1938 and, following a family conference, he was shipped off to Batavia, now Jakarta.

In Batavia he went to live with the family of one of his mother's male relatives, Zainul Arief, commonly called Pak Zainul, who had a reputation in the family for straightening out its young men and was a senior staff member in a Dutch shipping company. One of Zainul's daughters, Ratnah, would later become Idrus's wife.

Idrus and his wife "Ballroom Dancing" in the early 1950's

As well as being at home with Javanese and Sumatran culture, Pak Zainul's family was equally at home with the European musical and literary traditions of the middle- and upper-class expatriate colonial community. This broad cultural background was an important factor in Idrus's subsequent development as a writer.

Pak Zainul lived up to his reputation. Idrus settled down and did well in his studies and made plans to enter the medical school attached to the Dutch hospital in Batavia. However, these hopes died when the Japanese landed in the Dutch East Indies on January 10,1942. The Dutch surrendered two months later, and Idrus's formal education in Indonesia came to an end.

Idrus resented the Japanese bitterly. They had ruined his future prospects and those of his patron as well. Pak Zainul was ruined; the economy collapsed as the Japanese stripped the country of its assets. The Japanese military government banned the use of Dutch and all higher education in the Indies, which depended on use of the Dutch language, came to a halt. The only positive benefit of this ruling was more widespread use of Indonesian.

With his prospects of further education at an end, Idrus left the impoverished Pak Zainul's home, went to live with another of his uncles, and began the search for work. He managed to get a job with the publishing house, Balai Pustaka, which had been established by the Dutch in 1908, but after the Japanese takeover was allowed by the Japanese to continue under close supervision.

Here the young Idrus began to discover his literary talents and was encouraged to develop them. Idrus owed his job at Balai Pustaka to the fact that he had a formal education and had attained good marks, especially in languages. He worked in the editorial office, under the watchful eye of the Japanese censor. His early work was published in magazines that the publishing house produced.

Idrus was an eye-witness to the terrible effects of the Japanese occupation, and they provided him with the subject matter for his first collection of stories, *Sketches from the Underground* (*Coret-coret di bawah Tanah*). He also wrote a play, *Evil Takes Revenge* (*Kejahatan Membalas Dendam*), and somehow managed to gather a group of young amatures to rehearse and present it. The rehearsals went well until the parents of his actors, members of the city's older, moneyed and aristocratic families, read the play. They were shocked by the frankness of the language, which offended all canons of decency and good taste, and they refused to allow their upstanding young sons and daughters to appear in it. The play languished, unperformed.

By the time World War II ended in August 1945 Idrus had

already committed himself to the task of helping to fashion the new state. One of his good friends during this time was Chairil Anwar who was to go on to become Indonesia's leading poet, only to die tragically young, in 1948. Together with a number of other young writers, they were later to be grouped together as the "Angkatan '45", or the "Generation of '45".

On August 17, 1945 Indonesia declared itself to be an independent nation. Less than a week later, on August 22, the Japanese announced their surrender and, over the next two months, Allied forces began to arrive in Indonesia to supervise the return of the country to Dutch control. The Allies found that in many places Indonesian Republican forces had taken over key installations and had no intention of handing them over to the Allies, much less the Dutch.

Idrus and family - Kuala Lumpur Airport 1965

Balai Pustaka, free at last from the Japanese censor, and now for a short time under Indonesian control, put out a new magazine, *Pantja Raja*, and it became one of the means by which the work of Idrus and Chairil Anwar and others were to find an audience. Newspapers sprung up everywhere. One of them was *Merdeka* and Idrus soon became a member of its staff. By the time the British landed in Surabaya on October 25, the Republican militia had been armed by the sympathetic local Japanese commander and were skirmishing with Dutch nationals and their

Eurasian sympathizers who were seeking to regain control. Full-scale fighting broke out and before long Idrus found himself there, in East Java, as a *Merdeka* correspondent. He was stationed in the hill city of Malang but also worked on the front line around Surabaya. Later, when the Dutch took control again in Batavia, Idrus went back to writing and editing for the Balai Pustaka stable of magazines.

Idrus's future wife, Ratna, Pak Zainul's daughter, was still a student when independence was proclaimed in 1945, but after graduation she trained as a kindergarten teacher. She taught for two years and then went into radio and worked as a broadcaster. She subsequently joined the staff of Balai Pustaka and went on to combine broadcasting and editorial work. In 1948, when she and Idrus were both working at Balai Pustaka, they married.

That same year Idrus collection of stories *Dari Ave Maria ke Jalan Lain ke Roma* (*From Ave Maria to Other Roads to Rome*) was published to great acclaim. From the time of its publication until the present this book has been constantly in print, either in Indonesia or Malaysia. The book contains his story "Ave Maria" and the play *Evil Takes Revenge*, both written during the early Japanese period, as well as *Sketches from the Underground* and three other stories, including "The Story of a Pair of Shorts (*Kisah Sebuah Celana Pendek*)", "Surabaya" and "Another Road to Rome (*Jalan Lain ke Roma*)".

As becomes apparent from a reading of this collection, Idrus was a storyteller who wrote mostly about ordinary people who were distinguished only by some odd characteristic, circumstance, or misfortune. He did not deal directly with the larger issues on which many of his contemporaries and predecessors focused; instead, he dealt with simpler human themes.

In 1951, Idrus decided to fly with his wife to Padang, a place he had not visited since before the war and one she had never seen. At the time, in addition to his editorial and journalistic work, he was broadcasting short stories on Sunday mornings on Radio Jakarta and it seemed like a good idea to do some pieces based on post-revolutionary life in Padang and the surrounding area. However, even as the plane flew in and he looked over the crumbling, rust-roofed city, his heart began to sink. The city of Padang was experiencing severe depression. Economic recovery since the Dutch re-occupation in 1947 had been minimal. Idrus' somber mood did

Idrus (far left) with friends - Kuala Lumpur 1965

not lift as he went around the town looking up family members and talking to the local people. He found it impossible to write the kind of upbeat, innocuous and politically correct pieces the authorities expected and later, when his broadcasts were aired, the authorities threatened him with jail if he did not begin to change his tune.

In the story "Another Road to Rome," Idrus described the fate of a young man, Open, whose mother had raised him to always be frank and open in his dealings with others. As is seen in the story, however, in real life such frankness does not always sit well in polite society and can lead to numerous misunderstandings. Idrus described his style of writing as "*terus terang*" which may be translated as "candid" or "frank and open"; writing this way at the time was bound to get him into trouble.

A significant element determining how and what Idrus wrote was his own independent spirit. Further, the memory of his grandfather's financial ruin had not left him, and he remained constant in his hatred of feudalism. At the same time, he showed little inclination to toe an orthodox party line of either the right or the left.

Increasingly, in the late 1950s and early 1960s, it became almost a political necessity for an author to demonstrate leftist tendencies if he wanted to be both politically correct and successful. Idrus would have none of this, however. He went his own way and no orthodox ideology would hold him. Idrus was an omnivorous reader with catholic tastes. His style had been affected by the Indonesian and European influences to which he had been exposed in his youth, particularly in Pak Zainul's cosmopolitan household, as well as by his subsequent reading. He was familiar with the 20th century Dutch poet, Slauerhoff, and refers to him in his short novel *Aki* (1950). He translated the Flemish writer Willem Elsschot's novel *Cheese* (*Kedju*). He read the Americans of the post-World War I period — Steinbeck and Hemingway, for example, but he admired far more the work of the classic Russian writers, such as Dostoyevsky and Tolstoy and the post-revolutionary experimental writer, Ivanov; the Czech, Kafka; and the French writers Zola and Gide.

"Surabaya," one of Idrus' most popular pieces, combines factual reportage, either observed first hand or gained from those who were on the spot, and fictional episodes that were based on fact but reworked to heighten their impact and significance. No individual or group is depicted in heroic terms; all the participants are presented "frankly and openly." Idrus always wrote with his sharpest pen when he referred to people who thought of themselves as "big shots." In the story East Java's governor and a puffed-up, big-city journalist drop into the war zone for a quick look-see and are both nicely skewered.

Idrus in front of his house with his wife and children - Melbourne Australia, 1978

After his return from Padang, Idrus began to widen the scope of his activities. Prior to this, while the revolutionary struggle was still going on, he was employed by the army high command to translate military manuals. He found himself working day and night and his health suffered badly. Now that the war was over he continued with his translating work, not for patriotic reasons, but to help pay the rent. He worked for Unilever, the international business firm, he began to co-edit the monthly literary journal *Kisah*, the purpose of which was to provide an outlet for new fiction, poetry and criticism.

During the latter half of the 1950s the Indonesian Communist Party's influence had grown steadily, both directly and indirectly, through Party-affiliated organizations. One of these was Lekra, an acronym for Lembaga Kebudayaan Rakyat (The Institute for People's Culture), one of whose founding principles was "politics is the commander," meaning that art and literature are but tools for the development of a people's democracy. In promoting this view Lekra supporters often criticized, or even denigrated, the work of independent-minded writers. The poet Chairil Anwar, for example, might have been admired as a stylist but he was regarded as ideologically unsound. This was equally true of Idrus.

By 1960 Idrus could see no future for himself and his family in Indonesia's politically-charged environment. He and his wife decided to get out. They sold everything, and took their five children to Malaya, where they settled in Kuala Lumpur in 1961. There, from a distance, he watched events in Indonesia unfold. He put together a small collection of stories entitled *With Open Eyes* (*Dengan Mata Terbuka*) which was published by Pustaka Antara in Kuala Lumpur in 1961. With a light touch, the stories deal with corruption and the oddities and absurdities of everyday life in post-revolutionary Indonesia. One of the stories, "Why I Didn't Set Up My Own Business (Mengapa Saya tidak jadi Dirikan Perusahaan Sendiri)," describes the misfortunes of a man who gets caught up in the wheeling and dealing and corruption that marked many of the government's efforts to help indigenous traders and small businessmen. Another story, "A New Parliament has Opened in my House (Parlemen Baru dibuka di Rumah Saya)," describes the way the Indonesian parliamentary system of the 1950s was corrupted. Such stories could be given a wider audience now that Idrus was out of the country.

In Kuala Lumpur Idrus and his wife also opened a publishing house and together they published two magazines, one modeled on *Readers Digest* and the other specifically for children. In 1963 he published the novel *The Conscience of Mankind* (*Hati Nurani Manusia*), which was eventually republished in Indonesia in 1976.

In 1965 Idrus was offered a job at Monash University in Melbourne. He moved there on his own shortly afterwards. His wife and children followed one year later. During the years that followed, Idrus produced only one more book, a novel set in Australia, entitled *The Tale of Princess Penelope* (*Hikayat Putri Penelope*), which was published by Balai Pustaka in 1973.

During the 1970s Idrus's health began to fail, but there was one more literary interest that he was determined to explore which had grown directly out of his own ancestral roots among the Minangkabau people in Sumatra. After completing successfully his Master of Arts degree from Monash University he began, as part of his Ph.D studies, researching the storytelling traditions of the Minangkabau people, traditions which had been maintained over the centuries by *tukang kabar*, bards and minstrels, the time-honoured carriers of the word in all great literary traditions. His research took him back to his birthplace in Padang where he, a Minangkabau contempory bard, died suddenly, on May 18, 1979.

In his life Idrus had gone his own way, but eventually, in spite of his cosmopolitan experince and outlook, his Sumatran story-telling background had claimed him. It is tantalizing to reflect on how the new literary synthesis of East and West — towards which he seems to have been working — might have been expressed if he had lived to tell it.

Idrus looking older than his 56 years after suffering two heart attacks

IDRUS

Fujinkai

THE FUJINKAI WOMEN'S GROUP in the neighborhood was holding a meeting. The day before Mrs Sastra had been as busy as if she were marrying off her daughter, borrowing chairs, calling members. For Mrs Sastra this Fujinkai meeting was an important event in her everyday life.

"She's very enthusiastic," remarked one member to another.

Mrs Sastra stood to address the meeting and in a voice resembling that of a cat meowing in the cold, explained that she had been ordered by the authorities to call this meeting to discuss certain issues.

One of the members, sitting right in front of Mrs Sastra muttered, "Well, of course! If she hadn't been ordered to, she wouldn't have dared!"

Mrs Sastra glared at the woman, her expression as sour as the other woman's was scornful. She continued to speak with a slight quaver in her voice. And went on speaking for quite some time, though she failed to mention what the authorities had ordered her to discuss at the meeting.

Ten minutes, twenty minutes went by. All the members were yawning, like soldiers at a quiet battle-front, and still Mrs Sastra talked on. Her squirrelish mouth opened and closed like the hole of a bellows. Her nostrils flared like a fish-net in water, the black hairs inside resembling a squid's tentacles. Spittle oozed between her teeth and dribbled down her chin like snot from a child's nose.

Finally, one of the members stood. "Mrs Sastra, I must ask your permission to leave," she said with some embarrassment, "I have a lot of work to do at home."

The slight Mrs Sastra felt became apparent in her voice: "But why, Mrs Waluyo?" she asked angrily. "The meeting isn't over yet. We've just begun. And at home you work for yourself, while here we're working for the common welfare."

Mrs Waluyo thought on that but stated firmly, "I'm very sorry, Mrs Sastra." She looked at her miniature wrist watch. "But I have an appointment with the chicken-vendor at six o'clock. I'm trading some old clothes for a chicken." She nodded to Mrs Sastra and the other members, then made her way out.

As she was leaving she said between clenched teeth, "For the first and the last time! Common welfare, indeed!" she mocked.

Mrs Waluyo's departure left the other members feeling uneasy, like a divorced man who has suddenly come face to face with his former spouse.

The incident did not deter Mrs Sastra. She went on speaking, citing news articles that had appeared during the past few days, expressing appreciation to the Japanese navy for their brilliant victory on the seas east of Formosa, paying homage to the Japanese soldiers who had died as heroes on Pililiou Island, giving thanks for Indonesia's future independence to "The Empire of Greater Japan," and expressing thanks to the military government for how well its rice distribution program had been organized, with each person receiving one-fifth of a liter of rice per day.

Another member stood, this one a young woman who appeared to be right out of the village. She spoke Indonesian haltingly and her blouse was faded and threadbare. Her chest was as flat as the waters of Lake Toba, not a ripple anywhere. She coughed as she tried to make herself heard: "But Mrs Sastra, one-fifth isn't enough! Where are we supposed to get more? My man can't work. The Japanese cut his hands off because. . ." She seemed reluctant to finish her sentence, but she did want to strike some chord of pity in Mrs Sastra's heart. Maybe Mrs Sastra could help. She coughed again. ". . .only for taking a liter of rice from his boss' house. But he was forced to do it. Otherwise, my Salim is an honest man. Please help me, ma'am. My two children need more food. They're in the growing stage, you know."

All the members looked with pity at the woman, but Mrs Sastra's voice was firm: "I can't help you, Mrs Salim. The decision's been made and we have to obey orders. Times have changed. In the past we could question the authorities, but now is the time to obey. Besides, it's better this way. If things were now as they were before, the situation would never change. The Japanese do things differently! With them everything happens quickly. They've been here only two years, and we've already been promised our independence. But first we have work to do, Mrs Salim!"

Mrs Salim seemed on the verge of tears. "So it's down to one-fifth of a liter? Not even a quarter?" she asked in confirmation. "Then I had better get going. I got a lot of work to do at home."

As if just hearing an announcement of the Japanese military's defeat, Mrs Salim turned and walked slowly towards the door. Once she arrived home there would be no stopping her tears.

Mrs Sastra laughed derisively. "That's what happens when you let uneducated people attend meetings. They bring up irrelevant issues and ask irrelevant questions!"

Seated at some distance from Mrs Sastra, two other members, Mrs Joko and Mrs Surya, were busy talking among themselves: "My husband looks so poorly," Mrs Joko was saying to her friend. "I feel so bad, I don't know what to do. He works so hard and when he comes home all I have to feed him is rice-porridge. It's not so bad for me; food sellers pass by the house during the day. I can get *gado-gado,* fried *oncom,* or most anything to settle my hunger. Sometimes I spend as much as a rupiah a day. But my poor husband. . . !"

Mrs Surya, whose husband sat on the Shu Sangkikai advisory council which the Japanese had established, did not appear to share her friend's troubles: "For us, things are pretty much as usual," she boasted. "There hasn't been much change at all. My husband has a travel permit and can go anywhere he wants. If he goes to Banten he brings home coffee; if he goes to Cirebon he comes back with rice or Kooa cigarettes. Usually he brings back more than the both of us can eat. So what can I do? I sell it, and at seventy cents a liter, I make two rupiah, which is enough to cover the cost of seeing a picture show."

At this juncture Mrs Joko rose to speak to Mrs Sastra. "Excuse me, Mrs Sastra, but if this is all we're here to discuss at this meeting, then thank you very much, but I would like to leave."

The announcement came as a shock to Mrs Sastra. She fumbled in her handbag and took out a piece of paper. "Wait a moment!" she said to Mrs Joko. "What I was saying was only an introduction. The actual purpose of this meeting is. . ." She opened the folded piece of paper. "Here it is. . .that on December 8 it will be exactly three years since Japan declared war on the United States by attacking Hawaii. This event is to be commemorated, and the Fujinkai in the city have been given the assignment of visiting injured Japanese soldiers. For this, of course, we'll have to prepare some baked goods. And because that will involve some expense, well, ladies, let me put it briefly and say that the purpose of this meeting is to appeal to your generosity, and to ask you to contribute money for making cookies. At least two and a half rupiah per family — I don't think that's too much for you, is it? What's two and a half rupiah? Think of it as buying a liter of rice! I'm sure you won't feel it an imposition. Anyway I'll let you know later when we have to start work."

The Fujinkai members whispered to one another before one of them spoke up. "Two and a half rupiah is one thing but why did you have to give such a long-winded introduction just to tell us to dig even more deeply into our pockets? You can cross my name off the membership list of this Fujinkai right now! I don't care if people say that I don't have the right spirit."

"Mrs Samiun, please don't be so easily offended." Fear was evident in Mrs Sastra's trembling voice. "We must be patient. You misunderstand. I think I should tell you, even though it's supposed to be a secret, that everything I said came to me from higher up, together with the order to hold this meeting. And I worked very hard yesterday, Mrs Samiun, memorizing it all, word for word!"

Mrs Sastra wiped the sweat from her forehead. The meeting was adjourned without any further mishap.

TRANSLATED BY S. U. NABABAN

Oh...Oh...Oh...!

SUKABUMI IS KNOWN for its cool climate, but the people lined up in front of the ticket window were close to dying of the heat. Their backs, their necks, their armpits, their shirts were drenched with sweat. Alongside the row of humans, near their feet, flies as black as cough syrup gathered to feed on pools of spittle, some clear, some as thick as condensed milk.

From the crowd came the intermittent sound of a man coughing, hacking up phlegm and spitting on the ground. The flies swarmed around the newly fallen spittle like children fighting over freshly-fried bananas.

The person coughing was a young man, no fatter than a withered branch, standing towards the center the row.

"Why are you coughing?" the man behind him inquired. "It's not dusty here."

"I'd be coughing even in the cleanest of places," the young man answered. "I just got in from the Pacet Sanitorium. I'm heading for Jakarta."

The man who had questioned him pulled out his handkerchief. "If you have a chest ailment," he advised, "you shouldn't spit on the ground. That kind of thing is contagious, you know."

The young man coughed again, and from his mouth came a substance like clotted milk with a red spot in the center. It resembled the Japanese flag.

At the head of the line was an Indonesian man clad in little more than rags. His hand was pushed through the ticket window and he kept repeating over and over, "One fourth-class for Jakarta."

The ticket seller cast him an angry glance. "If you don't want to wait you can leave."

"I've been standing in line for half an hour," the Indonesian replied indignantly, "and I've still not been waited on! Yet you take care of that guy first." He pointed at a man standing behind the ticket seller.

The ticket seller shouted back: "What's it to you? That's my business. If you want help right away you can settle your business behind here, too. But that'll cost half a rupiah more!"

The Indonesian quieted down. He shook his head and grumbled to himself, "That's that, I guess. It's every man for himself these days." He then looked down at the bags of rice beside him. "...Even me," he added slowly.

A Chinese man moved out of line. Mopping the beads of sweat off his forehead with the folded tip of his handkerchief, he stepped to the head of the line to stand beside the Indonesian. This made the Indonesian angrier. "Excuse me, sir, but you shouldn't leave your place in the line. If you do that, everyone else will want to try. And then everyone will be pushing and shoving and making real trouble for the ticket seller."

"You talk too much," the Chinese man sneered. "Do you know who I am? I have a pass from the Japanese authorities." He then turned to the ticket seller. "One second-class to Jakarta."

The ticket seller was shocked. "But second class is only for the Japanese, sir, or for people with a pass from their district chief."

The Chinese man laughed and looked down at his fingers in which he held a five-rupiah note. "Here's my pass," he said. "The ticket to Jakarta is two sixty-five. The rest..."

The ticket seller snatched the money from the man's. "Here you are," he said with deference, "one second-class ticket for Jakarta."

THE TRAIN PULLED OUT of Sukabumi Station. In the second class coach the Chinese man was chuckling and smiling at a Eurasian girl. In the third and fourth class coaches passengers were jammed together. Some were complaining, some even crying because of the crowding.

When the conductor was making his way from the third- to the fourth-class coaches he stopped by a group of people huddled near the steps. "Tickets!" he demanded. When they proffered money instead his voice rose in mock anger: "What are you doing on the train? Why do you get on board if you don't have any tickets? How did you get onto the platform without them?"

"We gave something to the man at the gate," one of the party answered.

The conductor said nothing to this. He took the money from their hands and stuffed it into his pocket. "Next time," he warned them softly, "buy a ticket, okay?"

THE TRAIN CAME TO A STOP at a tiny station where several young men, all bare to the waist, got on. Only their caps identified them as *keibodan,* police auxiliaries. They searched the train for contraband. When finding someone's hidden bag of rice they confiscated it and took it off the train to the platform. They beat the smugglers, even the women.

One of the *keibodan* found a bag laying on a seat. "Whose is this?" he asked, even as his hand reached out to take it.

A police agent addressed the *keibodan* haughtily: "It's mine. If you want it, take it."

The *keibodan* immediately saluted. "Excuse me, sir, but I thought it was someone else's."

After their search the *keibodan* disembarked. Confiscated bags of rice lay in heaps on the platform.

"Is Mr Murakawa here?" one of the *keibodan* whispered to another.

The other man shook his head and mumbled between broad lips, "He just left for Bogor. Won't be back 'till this afternoon. We can divide the rice in five parts and leave one part behind to show we did our work today."

Just as the train was at the point of leaving, an Arab climbed on. "*Masya Allah,* God in heaven!" he exclaimed when seeing the dense crowd.

Behind the Arab came a young man in a tattered shirt and a wooden left leg. Limping, he attempted to climb on the train but there wasn't room for him inside and he was forced to hang from the doorway by the handrails.

"Where are you going?" the Arab asked. "Will you be able to hang on like that?"

"I'm going to Jakarta, sir." the young man answered politely. "There's no one left here who can afford to give alms. Maybe someone will get off at the next stop and I'll be able to get inside."

THE TRAIN WAS MOVING AGAIN. In the fourth class compartment the police agent was staring at a young woman with a hunched back. With a Don Juan sort of approach he asked her, "Pardon me, how old are you?"

"Huh, thirty-two," the woman answered in surprise. "Why do you ask?"

"It's nothing, but I was thinking what a pity it is that a woman as young as you is so hunched over." The policeman ran his hand over the woman's back. "Odd though, how smooth your hump is."

He appeared to give the matter some thought. "That's it!" he then declared. "It's rice, isn't it? Listen," he said to her, "I don't like to see a young woman so stooped. If you put your rice into my bag, when we get to Jakarta we'll measure it and I'll give you your portion back. Don't worry, the *keibodan* won't bother us any more."

The policeman laughed as the young woman shamefully pulled

the sack from her dress and poured the rice into his bag.

NEAR BOGOR, as the train was racing over the rails, the one-legged man hanging on to the door rails lost his grip and fell. Someone pulled the emergency cord and the train came to a stop. People ran back down the track, but the young man was dead. The conductor made some notes but left the body where it was. The train went on its way.

The Arab, witness to all that had happened, pulled out his handkerchief to wipe the sweat from his brow. "*Astaghafirallah,* May Allah forgive us," he intoned again and again.

An Indonesian, who was standing beside the Arab, had this to say: "It's better that he died here in this way than later on the banks of the Ciliwung in Jakarta."

OUTSIDE BOGOR the train stopped briefly at another small station. The conductor got off the train and hurried to a small house where there was a man waiting for him. The man had hardly caught sight of the conductor before he asked, "How did it go, Karim? All right?"

Karim nodded. "Yeah, all right, but only for one hundred and fifty rupiah. I'm hoping that you can give me my cut from that."

"I told you I wanted one hundred and fifty clear," the man advised. "That was three dozen genuine Koh-I-Noor. These days the market price is sixty rupiah per dozen. Here's ten rupiah for you but I can't give you any more."

Karim accepted the money and asked, "Got anything else for Jakarta?"

"Some penicillin. Is there a market for it in Jakarta?"

"There sure is, sir. All the young men in Jakarta have the disease. But don't make it too expensive."

The conductor returned to the train carrying several vials of penicillin.

NOT LONG AFTERWARD the train pulled into Jakarta's Gambir Station. The train's passengers pushed and shoved trying to be the first out of the building.

Outside the station's exit a young woman stood sobbing. When someone asked her what was wrong she could barely answer, "My rice. . . The policeman took my rice."

The people around her tried to catch sight of a policeman carrying a bag of rice but there was no policeman to be seen. And so the young woman kept on sobbing, till her tears were dry, as dry and empty as her purse.

TRANSLATED BY JAMES S. HOLMES AND HANS VAN MARLE

Surabaya

PEOPLE WERE DRUNK WITH VICTORY. Everything had exceeded their dreams and expectations. Their valor suddenly emerged like a snake from a thicket. Their self-confidence and patriotism bubbled over like the foam on a beer. Rational thinking declined, people acted like beasts, and the results were eminently satisfactory. People's faith in God declined. A new God had arrived, and was known under various names: bomb, machine-gun, mortar.

When some Eurasians dared to hoist the Dutch tri-color at the Yamato Hotel, the Indonesians were dumbfounded. The numbers of the dumbfounded grew and grew, and moved closer and closer to the hotel. A young man sprang forward, shimmied up the flagpole and ripped off the blue stripe of the Dutch tricolor. The Indonesians clapped and cheered, but the Eurasians were angry. They had not hoisted the flag for it to be torn down! They remembered how things had been three and a half years before, and they remembered their fathers, who had been real Dutchmen. They felt insulted, as though their own fathers had been stripped naked. This is what enraged them so. And when their anger was made concrete in upturned fists, a brawl ensued, just as in a Western movie. When the show was over, ambulances appeared; and after being loaded, they went slowly on their way.

The drivers appeared to drive with caution; their steering-wheels and hands were covered with blood.

At that time the Indonesians still believed in their old God. But when they began to feel the growing threat to their personal safety, they ravished the honor of the Japanese — their samurai swords and their guns — much like a rapist ravishing a young girl's honor. The Japanese moaned with pain and surrendered.

A new cowboy film appeared. Behind iron bars were yellow faces, and in the middle of the streets, cowboys with revolvers and knives at their hips. The revolvers were for shooting rustlers, and the knives for decoration. The girls didn't go for glittering titles or handsome looks: now they only had eyes for revolvers and knives, and willingly surrendered themselves to these murderous weapons. People walked about with swollen chests. No cattle were being stolen, but one could still hear shots every day. At first people were startled, but when they learned that these shots were aimed at the sky, at the home of the old God, they cheered happily whenever a shot rang out.

Then, one day, like a bolt out of the blue, the radio announced that the Allied Forces were about to land! People were shocked and afraid, as though anticipating great danger. One could sense uneasiness everywhere: in the people, in the cars roaring down the street, in the printing presses, and in the dogs. The dogs barked themselves hoarse till their voices were gone and their bellies collapsed like flat bicycle tires; no one remembered to feed them.

Everywhere people were saying the same thing: "The Allies aren't supposed to be our enemies, but they're killing and kidnapping people in Jakarta!"

And like a badly-trained choir they shouted: "We won't be treated like the people in Jakarta! We refuse such treatment! We'll fight! We've got revolvers and knives!"

Their shouts rent the sky, but the Indonesian leaders were also renting the hearts of the people: they were trying as best they could to explain to the people that the Allies would not act as they had in Jakarta. The Allies were coming only to take away the foreign prisoners-of-war and the Japanese. The people were split: one half believed what the leaders said, but the other half was still suspicious of the Allied Forces. Nonetheless they restrained themselves even as they watched the Allies land. The cowboys suspected that the Allied soldiers, Indians most of them and black as locomotives, were little more than bandits who had been given permission to run loose, and wreak their will like the late lamented Hitler. The whole community was upset. Nothing was safe: cattle, girls, gold, not even the cowboys' revolvers and knives. On the streets the cowboys were stopped by the bandits and forced to surrender their weapons.

"YOUR GUN OR YOUR LIFE!" the bandits shouted as they raised their bayonets.

But the cowboys refused to put up their hands. They weren't prepared to surrender their weapons, and they shouted back: "Take our lives!"

As they shouted, they began to fire. The bandits opened fire, too, and a fierce fight ensued, one that lasted a day and a night.

Then from Jakarta the chief cowboy and the chief bandit flew in. They held a meeting with local leaders. The result was a piece of paper full of English and Indonesian words beneath which were the signatures "Sukarno" and "Hawthorn."

The bandits relented. Thereafter their movements were restricted to the harbor area. The newspapers printed an important announcement: "We want peace, but we are prepared to fight. We have lost one thousand men. The enemy has lost three hundred!"

This succession of victories left people feeling even more intoxicated than before. Their faith in the new God continued to grow and they abandoned the old God entirely. They fell in love with carbines and revolvers, treating them like beautiful girls: they caressed them, kissed them, and sold them at very high prices. They beamed with happiness and pride. Their confidence in their own strength radiated from their rifle-butts and from their mouths. People were in wonderful spirits, just like the Romans the day before Vesuvius erupted. Their mouths stank of tobacco and hot air. Vesuvius was emitting fire and smoke. Any minute it would erupt.

For some days now the Allies had been landing more soldiers and tanks. The giant tanks rolled down from the ships like the Angel of Death himself descending from the sky: silently, and in secret. The smoke of Vesuvius grew thicker in billowing clouds. It was raining pamphlets from the sky: the Indonesians must surrender their weapons to the Allies! Just like God's command in the dreams of ancient Romans: "Romans, surrender yourselves to me, or I shall make Vesuvius erupt! I shall send down the Angel of Death to destroy you!" And just like the Romans, the Indonesians refused to obey and ignored the command. And the Angel of Death stalked the earth, roaring through his gigantic teeth. Vesuvius erupted. The Battle of Surabaya had begun.

Bandits dropped their bombs from the sky and pelted missiles from the sea. In no time at all thousands lay dead in the streets. The air was filled with thick, black smoke. Lightning flashed repeatedly. Flames licked at buildings and at the soul of Indonesia. . . .

2

THE ROADS OUTSIDE THE CITY were crowded with people, most of them women. Their faces showed their weariness and exhaustion from the long walk. Behind them were smoke, fire, cowboys, bandits, and everything they loved: their husbands, their burning homes, their European hens, their children and their spring beds. As they trudged along they cried like children, they whimpered. Some of the women gave birth and these lucky mothers felt overwhelmed by calamity. As they groaned with pain by the side of the road they cursed God. None of them wanted a child at this time. With swollen bellies they had fled from death, and now, in mid-journey, these bellies suddenly went flat, and one heard the cries of infants. There were few who bothered about what happened to these women. They walked on with heavy, leaden feet, heading for their primary goal: a safe town with a place to spend the night. The heat seared everything: leaves, and people's backs and throats. Leaves curled away from the heat, but humans could do nothing. They just trudged onward, in silence, everyone busy with her own thoughts.

One old woman had gone mad. She had not intended to flee. She had wanted to stay in the burning city, in her own beautiful home, seated beside her son-in-law's Erres radio and close to the safe where her gold was kept. Over and over she had said to herself: "I don't want to run away. I'd rather die here with my things!"

But when a bomb dropped near her house, she had run outside, and run and run, swept along in the stream of human beings heading out of the city. Now she was no longer normal; she seemed to be in a trance, unconscious of herself. With a smile on her lips she moved along with the others. She walked with swaying hips like someone going to a party. She smiled incessantly, and struck up conversations with those beside her.

She could not stop chatting: "Do you know Doctor Mustafa's wife? Oh, she's nice and friendly all right but has the bad habit of running down people behind their backs. Who is your husband? Always keep a close eye on your husband! There are very few men who never go to prostitutes. That's my experience. And what make of radio do you have?"

The old woman seemed not surprised at all when the woman at her side did not reply, but when an old man shouted, "Krian is up ahead!" she suddenly stopped short. She rubbed her eyebrows as if deep in thought then burst into tears.

"My things, my house, my radio!" she howled, and then began to run to and fro. She screamed senselessly. She tore off her blouse and her bra, discarded her batik wrap-around, and naked as Eve ran as fast as she could back in the direction of Surabaya and the feel of her belongings, especially her Erres radio.

In the sky, far above the refugees' heads, silver colored birds flew by. They roared loudly and dropped their filth — machine-gun bullets — as they flew on. The refugees scrambled for shelter in the gutters. They were as terrified of these birds as cats are of brooms. The filth that the birds dropped sank into the bodies of refugees, leaving burned-out holes. And then, as if the Angel of Death had done his duty, the birds disappeared.

The old man who had shouted that Krian was up ahead took a bullet in his right hand. He groaned in pain, pleading for pity and help from the other refugees. When several of the women came up to give him help, they suddenly burst out laughing and pointed at the man in pain. "Look!" they shouted to their companions, "He's not an old man! He's young!"

And no sooner had they yelled these words than they sprang on the man and tore off his coat, his wig, and his false mustache.

"Look at this!" they shouted once more.

The heat was parching dry and the sun bored through people's scalps. They were angry and suddenly as fierce as tigers.

"You swine! You coward!" they screamed. "While other young men are risking their lives, you're running away like a woman!"

Suddenly there was a howl which drowned all the others: "Kill him!"

Several women came up with large stones, which they dropped

on the young man's head. The man uttered one long last moan before the refugees continued their journey towards a safer town.

A well-known journalist from Jakarta arrived, intending to look into the conditions of the refugees. With the man's thin chest and bony buttocks, everyone who saw him knew that he had never been active in sports. More likely than not he frequently played with himself. But he had a sharp mind and, in a rather condescending tone, asked a doctor, "How many refugees were victims of the Allied machine-guns?"

The harried doctor did not like his work interrupted. "I'm not a statistics bureau!" he answered in annoyance. "Count them yourself!"

The journalist felt insulted by the doctor's impudence. His answer had left him with a bitter taste in his mouth. He looked around him and spotted a number of pretty female refugees. "Lots of opportunities here!" he thought. "A veritable heaven!"

Nonetheless, by the time the journalist returned to Jakarta he had completely forgotten these women. It was the sharp words of the doctor that echoed in his mind. In his newspaper, he had this to say: "The medical care given to the refugees is very bad. Few of the doctors realize the seriousness of our struggle!"

The refugees spent the night in Krian. There were not enough places to stay. Most slept on the platform at the railway station, some as straight and rigid as wooden beams, others curled in a fetal position.

During the night they began to dream out loud. Their dreams were of beautiful and pleasant things. A young woman sighed with pleasure in her sleep. "Now, now, be good. . ." she moaned. "People might see us!"

In one corner a woman was sitting up, unable to sleep. She cradled a bundle in her arms, swinging it rhythmically to and fro. Softly she sang a lullaby. When she wearied of singing, she began to speak: "Do you want some milk, my pet?"

She opened a bottle of milk with her right hand, but as she put the lip of the bottle close to her bundle, something startled her. Everything in her arms fell to the floor: the bottle of milk and a bolster. She stared at the bolster on the floor for a long time, then began to scream and sob: "My baby! My baby!"

The woman's screams caused the people sleeping near her to stir but by the time they had reached consciousness, the woman had vanished into the darkness outside the station. The bleary-eyed refugees stared at the shattered bottle of milk and the bolster. They looked around perplexed. Who had screamed? A bolster and a bottle of milk. But then they went back to sleep, very soundly.

3

TUMINAH FOUND A SMALL ROOM with her relatives in Sidoarjo. It was not an ordinary room. When these relatives had been less well off than they now were, the room had been used for storing charcoal and old bits of furniture. At that time the room had the smell of rotten fruit. When the relatives subsequently became a little richer, they used the room as a kennel for their newly-acquired dog. And now the lingering smell of rotten fruit was compounded by the smell of dog turds.

The lady of the house had no children of her own; that's why she purchased the dog. One thing she didn't do was to hold the dog in her lap like a baby, but she did set up a signboard in front of the house with a picture of a dog's head and the warning, "Beware of Dog!" When seeing the board, passers-by, including beggars, would suddenly become alarmed and hurry away. The lady of the house would laugh in delight at the sight.

"The dog is a faithful animal!" she would declare, as if repeating a lesson from elementary school.

Then the Battle of Surabaya erupted. And now Tuminah arrived at her relatives' house, exhausted by the fifteen-kilometer walk and her lack of food, hoping for a place to stay. The relatives hesitated for some time before they offered her the dog's room. They were very fond of their dog, yet custom required that they take pity on Tuminah.

So, while inwardly cursing custom, the lady of the house presented her brusque offer to Tuminah: "You can have the room, but you'll have to clean it up yourself. There's no bed and we've got no money, so don't expect anything from us. You can try to get a job tomorrow."

The lady of the house said a great deal more, but Tuminah did not hear. She felt blind and deaf from exhaustion and, at this point, could care less what people were saying. All she needed was a place to lie down, if only for that one night. As to what she would do the next day, she would wait to think about that.

When Tuminah opened the door of the kennel the dog began to bark but she did not hear it; she didn't even notice the dog.

The stench of rotten fruit and dog turds wafted through the air and into Tuminah's nostrils, but she smelt nothing. All she could focus on was an empty space on the floor, one exactly the size of her body. There she lay down and soon was snoring like a water-buffalo. At her feet and near her head were little heaps of dog turds. The dog contented itself by licking Tuminah's forehead.

Meanwhile, in the dining-room, the lady of the house was entertaining guests. Laughter was in the air, but when conversation turned to the Battle of Surabaya the lady of the house frowned. She spoke with deep emotion: "We must work together and help one another. We should give as much aid to the refugees as possible. If we have three pieces of clothing, we should be willing to give them one."

After saying this, she laughed loudly and the serious expression disappeared from her face.

IN THE TOWN where the largest number of refugees had gone, charitable organizations set up two barracks: one for female refugees and one for elderly males. The organizations had arranged it so that the occupants of both barracks would receive equal amounts of food. But when female refugees began going off with the guards to certain dark places beneath the dim rays of the moon, the distribution of food rations became heavily weighted towards the female barracks. The old men protested to the authorities, and waited hopefully for the results. And indeed the next day the results became evident to the elderly man, especially each elderly belly, for on that day the men received no food at all.

The barracks guards roared with laughter. "Don't make protesting a habit!" they advised. "You got to do as the women do! They surrender themselves to fate — and get even more food than they need!"

The old men fumed in silence. "How wonderful it must be to be a woman," they thought. "You can have both fun and food."

But finally they did scream at the guards: "You're swine! Swine! All of you!"

The female refugees received more and more food, and more and more love, from the guards. They became more abandoned by the day, often times forgetting the husbands that they had left fighting in Surabaya as they indulged in pleasures with the guards. There, in the barracks' dark places, many of the young women lost their most precious possession, but they did not regret it. During the previous weeks their suffering had been almost unbearable. How many kilometers had they had to walk, thirsty and hungry? So now that pleasure offered itself, why should they turn it down? After all, human beings are only human! They can bear almost anything, but afterwards they want some fun. In the women's barracks new and dirty words were born every day and, after several months, babies as well.

REFUGEES FROM SURABAYA were to be found all over Java. Those who tried to maintain former principles ended up living like rats on a ship who, when a big wave came, were dashed against the ship's sides and killed. Others lived lives of pleasure, seeking the short way out, working as call-girls in hotels or beggars in the streets. As if they had no hope for the morrow, they lived for the day.

One young man, Amat by name, had managed to escape from the clutches of the Allied soldiers and now boasted about it wherever he went. He refused to be called a refugee: he was a fighter who had become a refuge only after all his friends had been killed. He could tell you how mortars were loaded, what a machine-gun looked like, and how he had managed to kill ten British soldiers single-handed. To make the story more convincing he would add that he had killed them with a hand-grenade right smack on the target.

At first people listened to Amat with interest in his stories, but later they began to look at him with boredom and disgust, as if he were a used-up prostitute.

ONE OLD MAN CRIED in his room every day, like a small child who had lost something.

He was a man who had never loved his wife. "I can't be completely frank with you," he would often say to his friend, "But I can tell you there's something very unpleasant about my wife."

That might be the reason he had forgotten to bring her along when he fled from Surabaya. At first he had thanked God the All-Merciful for he felt like someone just released from years of suffering.

But when, as a refugee, he began to find life very difficult he also began to weep uncontrollably.

Over and over, all day long, he would shout: "Forgive me, Jaleah! If only you were here, my suffering wouldn't be so unbearable!"

At night, in his dreams, he would see his wife Jaleah, flirting with the Gurkha soldiers. "No, Jaleah! Please don't!" he would cry out loud.

4

IN THE FACE OF ENEMY CANNONS people were brave enough, but how terrified they were of enemy spies! This terrible specter raged like a hurricane through cities and through the hearts of men, leveling everything in its path — courage and rationality alike. Everyone suspected everyone else, and to free themselves from this specter's torment, they killed one another.

At railway stations near the battlefront all train passengers were forced to disembark. The men were sent to one room, and the women to another. These rooms were not medical clinics, but inspection rooms. Both the men and the women were stripped naked, like Adam and Eve, and searched all over, even in those places which people are usually ashamed of exposing, to see if they bore marks of being enemy spies. At first, the inspectors for the women had been young men who found themselves speechless and spellbound with lust. But after several women's organizations protested to the authorities about this barbarous behavior, the young men were replaced by elderly matrons.

One day the inspectors caught a male spy. The station-guards swarmed around the inspection room, cheering happily like children who had just been given candy.

"Kill him! Kill him!" they shouted in unison.

The enemy spy was pale as a corpse. As more and more people swarmed into the room, he stopped denying the allegation. He resigned himself to God and to the throng of the people.

A confused babble filled the room but one voice rose above all others: "Kill him!"

"But how?" someone asked.

"Shoot him!"

"No, that's too quick and too easy! Let's hang him!"

Then, like thunder, other voices resounded: "Let's drag him behind a locomotive!"

Then, suddenly, the voices fell silent, like a radio dying when there's a short-circuit in the house. In the doorway stood the stationmaster.

"What's the matter?" he asked calmly. "What's going on here?"

A number of station attendants answered in unison: "We have an enemy spy! Let's kill him!"

"Best not to take matters into your own hands," the stationmaster said as he walked into the room. "We must report this to the police."

Many in the crowd disagreed; their voices grew louder and louder with disapproval.

One young man stepped forward and shouted, "Impossible! The police aren't radical enough. Let's just kill him."

"Yes, kill him!" others began to shout. "We don't need to turn him over to the police. We're the radicals. We are the people! We are the people's sovereignty"

And like a reflex action, hands suddenly grabbed the clothes of the enemy spy. At first they beat him on the head with their bare fists, then they used pieces of wood, bits of railway tracking, and finally their machetes. Blood spurted from the victim's ears, nose, and mouth, reddish-black in color like the color of a ripe mangosteen. The man's brains oozed from his skull, white and runny like chicken marrow.

IN MODJOKERTO, A YOUNG WOMAN was walking through the market. Now and then she smiled to herself. She had just got married and was now going to buy some food for her husband. She always smiled to herself when she was doing something to please her husband. She loved him very much.

Suddenly, the woman's smile vanished. A man was standing in front of her with a revolver at his waist and a knife in his hand.

"Come with me!" he ordered.

Astonished and alarmed, the woman followed the man to the back of the market. There she saw more young men wearing revolvers at their sides, like Japanese military police.

One man stepped forward from the group. "Who's that you've brought here, Karto?"

Karto smiled. "What else?" was his simple reply.

On hearing this, the other men began crowding around the young woman who, by this time, was as pale as chalk. Her thoughts flew to her husband. For a moment she thought they were going to rape her, but then she abandoned this suspicion. Rapists don't usually want company, she reasoned.

Suddenly, a question was spat at her: "You're an enemy spy, aren't you?"

The woman was now completely bewildered. She wanted to answer but her lips seemed to be locked by fear. She could only shake her head, like a horse trying to shake flies from its neck. She tried to smile but when the men saw the smile they grew angrier still.

"Look! She's trying to win us over with a smile. That's what they always do, isn't it? Look at her with her red scarf, white blouse and blue slippers. She's a walking Dutch flag, and she doesn't think we don't understand their methods!"

All blood drained from the woman's face. Now she understood why she had been taken for a spy. She looked first at her scarf, then at her blouse, but when she bent to look at her slippers she was struck from behind and knocked to the ground.

Her nose was bleeding but that didn't stop several more blows from descending on other parts of her body. Curses filled the air until, suddenly, one of the men shouted in surprise: "Stop, stop! We're wrong! Her slippers aren't blue. They're black!"

Several in the group pushed the man aside to get a better look. "Come on, Parman! You're color-blind!"

But as they were about to resume their beating, the police arrived on the scene, fully armed. The young men acted as if they knew nothing, but the police took several of them to precinct headquarters, while the young woman was taken to the hospital more dead than alive.

When she came to, she told the nurse, "I've forgiven them. They're young and they're fighting for our country."

But the police were of another opinion. Fighting for one's country is fighting for one's country, but crime is to be punished!

5

PEOPLE HAD BECOME LIKE PACK-HORSES. They endured great suffering without complaint, and without understanding why they had to suffer so. Everything had become blurred in their minds: the future and the national struggle which had given birth to despair. The only thing that still stood out clearly in their minds was that they had to kill and drive out the enemy who were trampling on their newly liberated fatherland. And this they were doing with steadfast hearts, burning spirits and near-empty bellies.

The city was burning, like the tragic house in *Rebecca*. Smoke came off scorched beams like smoke from Zipper cigarettes while from people's mouths came the moans of death. The air stank of cordite and of human and animal carcasses; the hospitals stank of ether and rose-water. Intermittent explosions filled the air and were followed by clouds of black smoke. Even the rain was black and full of soot that burnt both ones eyes and heart.

The further the Allied forces penetrated into the city, the further the Indonesian Army retreated. But such is war! The strong advance, the weak retreat and die. Religious people will say that the strong are rewarded with victory by God, because they fight for justice. To reinforce this point they add that if the strong do not tread the path of justice, then no matter how strong they are, God will visit them with defeat and destruction. But twentieth-century generals do not share this opinion: they have more faith in cannon power than in superstitious dogma.

The attention of the entire people of Indonesia was concentrated on the battle now raging in Surabaya. Every time they heard that this or that building had been destroyed, they would sigh sadly, like a parent insulted by his own child.

From their lips came words no one could deny: "In time those buildings will have to be repaired. But for now, it doesn't matter."

LEMPER CAKES CAME INTO THE CITY from all directions. Wrapped in banana leaves and round as grenades, the rice cakes gave the soldiers a good laugh.

"This is how we're going to stop the British tanks!" they chortled as they hung the *lemper* from their belts. Later, at the height of battle, they would throw the cakes into their mouths.

One day Indonesian antiaircraft guns shot down several enemy planes and, suddenly, it was as if the world had been rudely awakened from its sleep. Telegraph operators around the world were busy, and in that day's papers an important news item appeared: "Indonesian Fighting Skill Compares with Germany!

This news made the Indonesians very happy; their fighting spirit bubbled over and their self-confidence returned. But no sooner did the enemy's giant tanks move firmly forward than everything disappeared: glowing spirit, self-confidence and hundreds of lives. A last smile on their lips was all the Indonesian people and their Army had to give the Angel of Death.

About those who remained alive after facing the Angel of Death people had to say, "They must be just like the President: immune!"

THE ARMY KNEW that their struggle to defend Surabaya would end in defeat. And they knew that the reason for their defeat would not be negligence, weakness of spirit, or because the Allied soldiers were braver. For that matter, it would not be boasting to say that their courage was twice as great as that of the Allies. They were able to capture ordinary-sized tanks from the enemy with bamboo spears, but those huge twenty-meter tanks and those airplanes with all the filth they were dropping. . .that was behind their defeats. And that is why they hated those murderous objects. And their hatred was enormous, as enormous as their hatred of imperialism.

When the peak of the battle came, the Army commanders came together for a meeting. They arrived with hearts filled with hatred and grief. Circles ringed their eyes from lack of sleep.

The meeting was conducted in a very democratic fashion, very much like a boys' club meeting. An observer could easily have forgotten that he was not in the midst of booming cannons and mortars. The meeting's chairman described at great length the course of the struggle in the past few weeks. He didn't forget to mention that he should in fact be in Malang where his wife was preparing to give birth. "And thank God that there are still babies being born," he added. "Otherwise, seeing how many people have died here, we would certainly give up hope."

He smiled sadly as he continued: "But I am not going to join my wife. Let the babies be born in safe places. We who are here will die. There is a balance to everything. I've sent my wife a letter as well as my share of the *lemper* for the newborn child."

At the end of the meeting it was decided to accept the chairman's proposal that they all die together in Surabaya. After all, as the reasoning went, more babies were being born in safe areas anyway. They would hold out to the last drop of blood.

Suddenly, amid all the pleasure derived from making the decision to die, one of the officers had an inspiration, an excellent idea indeed. As this man unfolded his inspiration to the assembled group, his thoughts were not in Surabaya but flying high above the Netherlands. He saw the Netherlands being flooded as the German fascists set about forcibly occupying the country. And though Germany had eventually managed to occupy the Netherlands, a large number had been killed in the inundation.

In a loud clear voice he asked those present: "What do you think of us doing the same thing here, to keep the Allied fascists from entering our country?"

Other officers put forward their own ideas. One suggested that at this critical juncture the whole Indonesian people, seventy million strong, be urged to line up and march against the giant tanks and let them run over their bodies — all seventy million of them!

"The tank-drivers would get tired of mowing down so many bodies. They'd die of exhaustion, and we could grab their tanks!"

Another officer suggested that within the next two days the government order giant tanks of its own from abroad. When another officer asked how the tanks were to be transported in such a short time, the officer replied: "By plane! From Australia and the United States it's only two days by plane, right?"

The officers burst out laughing. The proposal was turned down without a vote. At the end of the three-hour meeting they accepted the proposal to inundate Surabaya as the Dutch had inundated the Netherlands. Furthermore, all the officers present swore to die on the field of battle, since in safer places babies would go on being born, by the thousands, by the millions.

6

THERE IS A SAYING that a good businessman is so good at lying that he can no longer tell whether he's lying or telling the truth. And real criminals never dirty their own hands with crime. What they do is routine, nothing out of the ordinary, like a clerk's job in an office. That people might suffer from their activities doesn't concern them at all. Such things happen, or so go the workings of a bureaucratic mind.

In the end all the refugees found a roof for their heads: in hotels, barracks or kennels. The newspapers didn't say much about them. One could have got the impression that they no longer existed, however a warning issued by a certain ministry served as a reminder: black-marketers were to stop turning female refugees into prostitutes with their piles of money.

The black-marketers themselves had a good laugh when they read the announcement. Why should the ministry interfere in sexual matters? Would the French Ministry of Information try to ban growth in the number of prostitutes in Paris? Wasn't it a normal thing in this world for there to be women who became prostitutes, just as there were people who became literary scholars? For scholars one built big schools and universities; for prostitutes one built large houses. And wasn't it normal for everything to have its own price? Government ministries should take care of their own problems, like making five-year plans, and not dirty their hands with prostitutes! The black-marketers laughed loudly — and the number of prostitutes increased daily. Soon it reached the point where you could no longer tell the ordinary women from the special ones — just like the businessman who can no longer tell whether he's lying or telling the truth.

Among the female refugees there were some, to be sure, who remained faithful to both their religion and their husbands and refused to be bought by the black-marketers. These women, when invited by black-marketers to leave the straight and narrow path, prayed to God seven times a day and refused the invitation with a bitter smile. That they could still smile, even if it were bitterly, was thanks to the guidance of their husbands who were meeting their death under the giant tanks.

But the pious women had to keep themselves alive, too, and this required money which was not something they could ask God for, even if they prayed thirteen times a day. And since the government could not supply them with what they needed, certain gods appeared on the scene, kindhearted and compassionate, from some never-never land. These gods went in and out of the neighborhoods, looking for refugees, especially those who were in trouble. Wearing sweet smiles, these gods "gave" the refugees the money they needed. When the recipients of their largesse got up to fetch some tea, the gods would politely refuse: "Don't trouble yourself, ma'am. No need at all, sir. Please don't bother."

And true enough, at these moments the gods were not lying; they had no need for tea, or even for lemonade. There was only one thing they needed, a simple elementary-school problem in arithmetic: how to make ten into twelve? An elementary school pupil would add two new palm-twigs to ten old ones to get a total of twelve. But these gods did not have to add anything to anything. They simply waited until the number ten automatically became twelve.

There were, of course, people who disapproved of such usurious activities and who angrily voiced their complaint — "This is absolutely scandalous!" — even as they racked their brain, trying to think up a less scandalous method for increasing their wealth.

These people could often be found among the groups who organized food distribution for the refugees. There they did not try to figure out how to make twelve out of ten. Easier and less scandalous calculations occupied their minds, for example how to change two hundred grams into one hundred ninety five. How to change one hundred ninety five grams into one hundred ninety; one hundred ninety into one hundred eightyfive, and so on. It was never more than five little grams. In the end, however, the refugees were left with a ration no larger than would feed a bird.

When the outside world protested that the government of the

Republic was killing its own people, the government strongly denied it. It even announced its willingness to produce a list of the foodstuffs distributed to the people under its care. Officials at the Bureau of Statistics added that these figures were "live," capable of speaking for themselves. But the food situation in the barracks showed that these figures were "dead," with no more life in them than a painting. The only things which were capable of saying anything, and which were very much alive, were the people who made the calculations of how to turn one hundred eighty-five grams into one hundred eighty. And the only people who could make these people talk were the judge and the executioner.

As time went on people took an increasingly lively interest in the fate of the refugees. When it was learned that thousands of people were fleeing from Surabaya suddenly all the houses in nearby towns were fully occupied. Refugees with money scoured villages in search of a house, a room or a garage, but all in vain. But invariably, when they were on the verge of despair, one of the new gods would appear and, with kindheartedness and compassion, offer their assistance: "Housing is very difficult here; it's been that way for a good while now." At this point the god would then pause to watch the expression of the refugee who was trying to rent a house, exactly as a psychiatrist watches a patient. If the refugee showed despair, he continued: "But I've got a friend who's willing to give up his house to help refugees. All he's asking is a small sum to pay for the removal of his things."

And when the refugee asked what the sum might be, the god would mention a small figure, say "one," "two" or "three." Continuing to smile he would add that behind these figures three trivial little objects would have to be affixed: "zero, zero, zero." Thus, a small room might be "one" plus "three zeros"; a garage, two plus three zeros; a small house, three plus three zeros. These small sums would go to pay the moving costs of the people willing to give up their places to the refugees they pitied and who had suffered so much. They accepted these small sums of money with a feeling of sharing the sufferings of the refugees.

"In this time of revolution, we must stick together and help one another!" they would say in a low voice.

7

IN THE LAST MOMENTS of the battle to defend Surabaya, people again remembered the old God. Every evening on Radio Revolution, one could hear the traditional Islamic call, "*Allahuakbar!* God is Great!" But somehow, perhaps because God did not own a radio, or because He was tired of witnessing the behavior of human beings who remembered Him only in times of adversity, He failed to hear these sacred words.

The Indonesians suffered one defeat after another until the Allied Forces finally announced over their own program, "Surabaya is safe once more!"

The fight between the cowboys and the bandits was over, and this time the bandits won. But there were still gaping wounds and the people in Surabaya were still suffering. Buildings continued to go up in flames and those not on fire looked like piles of buffalo dung.

The Indonesians in Surabaya were ruled by the bandits and lived like soldiers on the front lines. At any time a stray bullet could pierce them, at any time they could be arrested, and at any time they could take their last breath. Before that happened, however, they would not surrender. Like the defeated Germans they did not bow down — quite unlike the Japanese when they lost the war. In their hearts they were proud, proud as the politicians had been when they were led off to prison by the Dutch.

A respected Islamic scholar went insane and died. Formerly he had been a bosom friend of the Japanese and had trusted them one hundred percent. But when the Japanese behaved just like the Dutch, showing themselves to be cruel and clever at giving empty promises, he began to distrust this dishonest brother. Even so, he did not raise his hand to beat his brother; he simply waited in silence for his brother to be "beaten to death" by the situation. But this moment came too late for him, and long before the Japanese were "beaten to death" he was taken to a lunatic asylum. When Indonesian independence was proclaimed, he seemed to improve a little and happily shouted "Freedom! Freedom!" along with the rest, but, alas, it was not for long. When the Indonesians of Surabaya began to act like cowboys in saloons, kissing both girls and revolvers, he suffered a relapse. He was unable to join other Surabayans in their worship of new gods. And when the city became "safe once more," his madness intensified and he died with his lips twisted in hatred and scorn.

THERE WAS A CERTAIN MIDDLE-AGED MAN who always hid his left hand inside his trousers pocket. Only when absolutely necessary did he take it out. But people never saw it bare; surprisingly, it was always wound tightly in a white handkerchief. Everyones curiosity was piqued. One day, someone finally asked the man about it: "Excuse me, but your left hand makes me very curious! When I think of it at night I can't fall asleep, and during the day I can't think or eat — it's got me as anxious as a man thinking about an unfaithful sweetheart! I keep asking myself, why is it always hidden? Why is it always wrapped up? Won't you free me from this mental torture and answer the question that plagues my heart?"

The man suddenly turned pale as chalk and spoke with considerable embarrassment: "It's nothing really. It's just that all five fingers of my hand are gone. Allied soldiers cut them off. That's why I always wrap my hand. Since I find the sight of my hand loathsome, I don't want other people to feel disgusted by the sight."

Now it was the questioner who felt ashamed, and he moved away. No one else thought to ask why the Allied soldiers had cut off the five fingers of the man's left hand. Had he stolen? Was he a looter? People didn't feel it necessary to ask. It was as though it were perfectly natural for the Allied soldiers to cut off people's fingers and slit people's throats.

YOUNG INDONESIANS NO LONGER ROAMED the streets as they had done in the cowboy era. Now they lived in an orderly manner in long buildings. Early in the morning they were already awake, and after consuming a tiny piece of hard bread, they clambered into British trucks which took them to various sites where they worked on important jobs for the country's development: sweeping streets, clearing up debris and serving as porters at the harbor. Told this way, one might think the young men performed these chores voluntarily. Such would be mistaken. If these young men rose early, it was because of the yelling and cursing of guards. When they went off to their jobs, there were always in the trucks several fully-armed Gurkha soldiers to accompany them. While some of the Gurkhas were kind and tried very hard to create a cheerful atmosphere, the young Indonesians could only smile bitterly and bow their heads in shame as they passed the people on the streets.

No, at that time these young people were not creatures with a will of their own: they were the Allies' "prisoners-of-war." They went about their tasks without complaint but in their bitter smiles one could see pure steel, the metal of freedom.

THERE WAS AN ADOLESCENT GIRL whose clothes were nothing but rags and would say to everyone she met, Englishmen, Gurkhas and Indonesians alike, "Hey! I'm not a virgin any more! See for yourself!"

Having said this, she would grope under her skirt and,

a seconds later, as if she were doing a magic trick, she would remove a dirty yellow rag from between her legs. The Englishmen would stare for a moment at the dirty yellow rag and then quickly turn their heads away, grinning knowingly at one other. The Gurkhas roared in laughter when seeing the rag, then would stare at it for minutes on end as if mesmerized by its spell. The Indonesians didn't look at all. Just hearing what the young girl said was enough for them to flush with hatred and revenge. They might mutter to themselves as they walked quickly on, "Another victim of the revolution!" Whose audible retort would be: "Just like you and me! Just like all of us, like all the Indonesian people!"

8

IN MAY OF THE NEXT YEAR, six months after the Battle of Surabaya had broken out, the newspapers in Malang commemorated the occasion by publishing in red ink.

But why red ink, people asked themselves. Was the Battle of Surabaya akin to Trotsky's battle against Czar Nicholas III? Or did it symbolize the Indonesian blood that flowed in that city?

No one knew the answer, not even the editors of the newspapers themselves. All they knew was that when they saw the red ink tears welled up in their eyes. Those who saw them cry naturally supposed that it was because they were reading some truly tragic story or because they felt sorry for all the young men, the nation's best, who had fallen in battle. But such an observation would have been mistaken, since those who had been crying soon wiped their faces and burst out laughing as they spat on the red ink as if it were a dirty and disgusting object.

IN MOJOKERTO THAT DAY work at the public kitchens was piling up. The commander of the local division had given orders for thirty thousand *lemper* to be prepared for the soldiers on the front line. In his letter to the head of the public kitchen he wrote, "Our boys at the front cannot celebrate this day of commemoration like the people in the towns. To keep up the spirit of our boys, I ask for your cooperation in sending them thirty thousand *lemper* with meat inside. I know that rice is hard to come by and that the price is very high. That is why I do not ask for rice, only for *lemper*."

At first the head of the public kitchen was proud to receive this letter from the Division Commander. "There's a real fighter," he said to the other committee members, "He knows that rice is hard to get. That's why he's only asking for *lemper*. I'm proud we have young men like him!"

But when he arrived at the market to buy the ingredients for the *lemper*, he learned that the price of sticky rice was higher than that of ordinary rice, while meat for filling the *lemper* was so expensive that the public kitchen's budget could not possibly afford it. Cursing the sticky-rice vendor and the meat-seller, he hurried back and shot off a letter to the division commander: "This letter is to inform you, sir, that the price of sticky rice is higher than that of ordinary rice. Because the public kitchen can not afford the meat to fill the *lemper* either, we are sending thirty thousand bananas to your soldiers instead. We pray, sir, that you will understand."

When the division commander received his banana, he tried banishing the taste of the almost rotten fruit by imagining that he was eating a *lemper* full of very delicious meat.

ASIDE FROM THE FACT that its newspapers were printed with red ink, Malang also organized an "Ocean Rally." Under the Japanese this kind of meeting was usually called a "Giant Rally," but after the objection of so many people, all of whom were one hundred percent anti-Japanese, the rally was given this new name.

Thousands of people thronged to the Malang stadium. They bore the heat of the sun very patiently, just as they had borne three hundred and fifty years of colonial oppression. But secretly they were annoyed.

When the national anthem was being played people stood erect as soldiers and all joined in singing of "Indonesia Raya." A shiver ran through people's necks. Everyones hair stood on end: on their necks and legs alike.

After the national anthem was over several genuine nationalists burst into tears. "This is what we've been fighting for all along," they cried hoarsely. "It's for this that we've sacrificed our material possessions and the lives of our young men. What a beautiful anthem. Our struggle has not been in vain!"

Suddenly everyone fell silent. All eyes turned to the front, to a small and stiff-looking white figure on the dais. From him came a voice that crackled like dry leaves; it was the deputy governor of East Java delivering a speech. There were many rumors about the deputy governor, some good, some bad, but as he described the situation in Surabaya the day before the battle, everyone listened openmouthed to his description of the Allied Forces' arrogance. As good or bad as the deputy governor was, when he went on to say that such insults could not be ignored, everyone agreed.

Next to speak was the division commander of Malang. Though elderly, he tried his best to put spirit into his speech and to talk like a young man: "I am a General not because of these insignia on my collar. I am a General because of the people, by the people and for the people! In the name of Allah, I am a people's General!"

After every speech the stadium burst into a roar of applause. It might as well have been an international soccer match the audience was watching. But after the division commander's speech the applause was followed by broad and scornful smiles: people had heard such words all too often. What people wanted now was something new, something vital; they despised anything old and stale.

The people began to applaud again, this time ten times more loudly than before. Something important was about to occur. All eyes were turned to the front, but this time their gaze rested not on a short white figure but was fixed on something dark-looking and dirty, on top of which was a tangle of hair as long as a woman's, and from which came the musty smell of a pillow never aired in the sun.

Bung Tomo, the voice of "Radio Insurrection" was speaking! At first he spoke very slowly in order to quiet the audience. His voice was loud and harsh though the man himself was petite, almost pretty. His eyes sparkled like the beam of a light-house far out at sea.

He spoke briefly but forcefully of his experience at the front: "There's only one thing I'm afraid of and this is female spies. A woman can be more cruel and more cunning than any man. When I walk through the streets of Malang girls look at me with seductive smiles on their lips. But remember this, all you girls out there, I will only take one girl, and she will be no enemy spy. No, as long as the revolution continues, I will remain single. And therefore I advise you not to waste your seductive glances. They will not melt this man's heart."

The thousands of people in the stadium roared with laughter and cheered their approval. The younger married men inwardly decided to emulate Bung Tomo and divorce their wives as soon as they got home. On second thought, however, they changed their minds. "After all," they said in consolation, "It wouldn't make any difference. My wife's certainly not an enemy spy!"

Hearing the roar of the applause, Bung Tomo instantly transformed. Suddenly he was like a wounded buffalo and in a loud and savage voice denounced the behavior of the Allies in Surabaya from the day they landed. His sparkling eyes seemed to hypnotize his audience as he described the cruelties the Allied soldiers had inflicted on the young Indonesian fighters they captured.

Eventually his throat grew dry and in one last fiery outburst he concluded his oration: "We must eradicate all swindlers: regular swindlers, swindlers of rank and bullets and military uniforms, and British swindlers too! We must continue the struggle! It's only been six months so far, but if necessary we shall to continue to fight for another sixty years! We must drive out the Dutch and any other foreigners who want to colonize us again!"

9

SURABAYA WAS COMPLETELY UNDER THE CONTROL of the Allies and was now "safe once more." The Indonesians could do nothing but at every moment, on every occasion, and with one hundred percent certainty, the Army leaders announced, "We shall recapture Surabaya — at the soonest possible date!"

But when they arrived at the front lines, they came face-to-face with a one-hundred-percent reality: the enemy's giant tanks were still there, the enemy's airplanes were still in use, and neither were going to be bluffed by boastful words alone. Further, the front was now no longer Tanjung Perak Harbor; it had moved deep into the interior.

Now and then there were minor skirmishes. Once again, as in the first days of the battle, rifle-, cannon- and mortar fire were common sounds. For the most part, however, the battlefield was silent, and this silence, which lasted for days and months, put a heavy strain on the troops' morale. Waiting was more demoralizing than a major battle. In a battle soldiers don't have time to worry about when a bullet is going to strike their chest; they don't have time to think about the grieving sweethearts they left behind. In short, in a major battle soldiers don't have to think at all. They act! Either they kill or, if the situation seems hopeless, run like hell to the countryside.

During these quiet days the Army leaders experienced many headaches: the soldiers' numerous requests, most of them impossible to fulfill. Finally, when they could stand the situation no longer, they sent off letters in every direction: "Dear sir. Please send us a theatrical troupe. Our boys can't stand this situation any longer. If you don't have a theatrical troupe, send something else, anything at all to break the monotony."

In fact the Army leaders knew exactly what the young soldiers wanted. To break the monotony the commanders had not asked for bananas or *lemper*. No they had requested a theatrical troupe. For in such troupes there are always some girls, and it was really girls that the soldiers wanted when they made their impossible requests.

The Army leaders also knew that a troupe would leave immediately after it had performed, but that the memory of the visit would not disappear nearly as soon as the thought of *lemper* or half-rotten bananas. Especially for the romantically inclined among the soldiers, the show girls would be remembered forever.

And a theatrical troupe was sent out. The troupe arrived in festive humor but when the Army leaders saw the cast, their faces turned as dark as the sky before a storm. "What are the people on the home front thinking?" they asked. "Are they crazy? Look at this: here were are, fighting to the last man, and they send us a troupe of dogs!"

But the ordinary soldiers were happy. They didn't care whether the girls were good-looking or not; it was good enough that they were girls! A girl at the front was like water in the Sahara desert. And since it was now the era of People's Sovereignty the Army leaders had to give in and to watch the ugly girls perform.

Later, when the next quiet period occurred, the Army leaders would send another request to the home front: "Dear sir. The monotony is growing unbearable once more. Please send us some *lemper* and bananas as soon as possible. If they are not available, send anything, so long as it is not a theatrical troupe!"

The front line around Surabaya was enormous. Besides the Army's guard posts there were also Red Cross stations, but these aside, there were only dense forests and oppressive monotony.

Because there were many pretty girls at the Red Cross stations, some people who were faithful to their religious beliefs, decided to establish a demarcation line between the men's posts and the girl's stations. On this demarcation line, between the men's posts and the girl's station, a signboard containing an announcement by the local Army commander was posted: "It is absolutely forbidden to cross this demarcation line without the permission of the head of the Army post or the head of the Red Cross station."

The demarcation line was guarded by several well-disciplined soldiers, a situation that continued for several weeks, until finally people got tired of being lonely and their sanity returned. "What is the army doing, guarding the young men and women," they asked, "when it should be watching the giant tanks, the airplanes and all the imperialist forces that would dominate our country?"

Accordingly, the guard at the demarcation line was abolished. The signboard vanished, too, and an atmosphere developed which consoled the lonely and made them forget such trivial things as battles, sweethearts left behind, and even death itself. For now the soldiers and the Red Cross girls were faced with fulfilling a more important duty, one more important than anything else in the world, namely, the continuation of the species!

At a session of the Provincial Assembly in Malang the commander of the division on the outskirts of Surabaya was severely criticized. One of the delegates was extremely angry because he had once been rudely stopped by the guards at the front. He urged that this fascist situation be remedied: "Our country must not become a militarist state," he said. "The Army must be subordinate to the officials of the civilian government."

Another member expressed his disappointment that many soldiers violated the rules of propriety. He disapproved of soldiers consorting with the Dutch female internees. "I don't mind if their goings-on take place in the dark," he said. "My children won't be corrupted by that. But I do strongly object to their consorting in the middle of the market-place." That, he concluded, was one of the factors behind the Army's defeats in the Battle of Surabaya.

Thereafter an Army representative was given the floor. His appearance was so dashing everyone would have been proud if the whole Army had his build and posture. At first the man spoke slowly, with carefully chosen words. But as he spoke, he became more and more impassioned. In the end, as a result of his speech, everyone condemned the criticisms of soldiers previously aired by members of the Assembly.

The Army representative's words were more or less as follows: "The state our army is in is pitiful indeed. Our boys have nothing but bamboo spears to fight with. Even so, they are standing their ground, and have even repelled the enemy's attacks, thereby saving all of us here on the home front. I won't deny the criticisms of my boys, in fact I want to add to your criticisms by telling you about a particularly pitiful aspect of the situation. . ."

He glanced at the female members of the Assembly before continuing: "Excuse me, ladies, but I don't want to beat about the bush. The pitiful situation I just mentioned is that at this moment ninety-five percent of the boys who are now bearing arms, ninety-five percent mind you, are suffering from a disease that will make your hair stand on end! These men have syphilis! Yes, syphilis, my friends! The Allies have been pouring out prostitutes near the front lines, and since our boys have been getting so little entertainment from the home front, naturally they've tried to find it from these whores. Now, my friends, I ask you, how can we rectify this situation? Please tell me how. We military men don't say much, but I hope you will understand that in our struggle we are faced with many difficulties: shortages of penicillin and other medicines and a surplus of criticism!"

The Assembly fell silent. Members who had previously uttered such sharp criticisms now felt very ashamed. A few of the delegates who had sons at the front thought to send cables to remind their boys to take good care of themselves.

A month later an intensive investigation revealed that the Army representative was, as it turned out, a man with a lively imagination who had given free play to his fantasy at the Assembly session. The investigation made it clear that no soldiers were fighting with bamboo spears and, most important of all, that the figure of ninety-five percent grossly exaggerated. Accordingly, at the next session of the Assembly, the same member who had once been rudely treated by Army guards mustered up the courage to rebut the Army representative.

He spoke in an angry voice: "We have made an intensive investigation of everything you said at the last meeting. It turns out it was all a pack of lies! All you wanted to do was to get us to stop making any more criticisms. I therefore hereby strongly propose to this Assembly that we urge the Army to eliminate lies and syphilis completely!"

The Assembly applauded their approval. In near unison they shouted, "Down with syphilis! Down with imperialism! Crush them both!"

TRANSLATED BY S.U. NABABAN AND BEN ANDERSON

The Shorts

ON THE DAY THE JAPANESE ATTACKED Pearl Harbor, Kusno's father bought his son a pair of dress shorts of thick drill — 1001 brand — made in Italy.

Kusno's father was ignorant of politics and was totally unaware of the attack's significance. The one thing he did know was that his son didn't have a decent pair of shorts to wear. On that day when Pearl Harbor was attacked anyone who knew anything about international affairs displayed some kind of reaction, whether it be hatred, fear, or anger. But not so Kusno's father who was smiling amiably; he had obtained what everyone had thought to be impossible: a pair of shorts for his son.

Kusno himself was almost fourteen, just out of primary school, and about to look for work. Dressed in new shorts, he had the impression that jobs would simply be waiting for him. He hoped to show his father that he was a son who knew how to repay his parent's kindness. In brief, that day, Kusno's family was happy as never before in living memory, and the news about Pearl Harbor, grave as it was, stirred not an echo in the hearts of these simple people.

How very true it is that only the great want war while the common people ask nothing more than to live in peace! Unfortunately for Kusno, he was unable to obtain a job as quickly as he had expected. Potential employers were all too aware of the gravity of the hour, that above the office buildings heavy clouds were massing, and through them was peering the Angel of Death. The inevitable result was "no hands wanted."

Kusno was forced to adjust his terms to the market. Since he could not be a clerk he would be a door-keeper. But door-keepers weren't wanted either, and after endless traveling from one office to another, he finally got a job — as a "boy," with a salary of ten rupiah per month.

Kusno's father was, to put it mildly, even less delighted about this than his son. He knew what being a "boy" meant. He was one himself. To see his child sinking into the same rut depressed him badly. When, in the course of time, Kusno had children of his own, would they, too, be "boys"? Generations of "boys," from father to son till the end of time? But as with other people who were forced into the same situation, Kusno's father recalled that while man proposes, it is God who disposes.

Kusno was a diligent worker who liked to dress neatly for work but, over time, because of frequent washings, his 1001 drill shorts began to lose their fine finish. Every month he counted on buying a new pair, but his ten rupiah a month were barely enough to keep him in food. As time went by he had to wash his shorts more and more, and each time he washed them, their appearance became all the more worrisome.

Kusno's thoughts were concentrated on his shorts. What was to become of him when he was no longer possible to wear the shorts? Daily he prayed to God that there would be no rain. But when it did rain Kusno regarded his shorts as a mother would gaze on her son about to leave for the war.

Heavy drill 1001. One, zero, zero, one. One multiplied by one equals one. But one minus one, how much does that leave?

Kusno had shorts on the brain, especially on days when he had no money to buy the soap he needed to wash his shorts.

No indeed, simple folk are never for war. All they want is a simple life, one without the fear of having no shorts to wear the next day. It was the higher-ups, the bigwigs standing behind this war: some for "democracy," others for the establishment of the"Greater Asian Co-Prosperity Sphere."

Kusno had no means of knowing what democracy meant but the word "prosperity" did catch his interest. For him it brought to mind his shorts. For him "prosperity" meant shorts. That is why, when the Japanese Army arrived he, too, welcomed them with hand-shaking and hugs.

Just as the Indonesian masses were to live dreaming of independence, for the next three years Kusno lived with the dream of obtaining a new pair of shorts.

But as with independence, new shorts became unimaginable. And when Kusno finally did give up the last thread of hope, his shorts were so threadbare they no longer resembled clothing. The short's fine white color had vanished long ago; what remained was now a confusion of dirty yellow spots. They were not fit for wear, not even by a "boy" such as himself.

When Kusno finally plucked the courage to ask his boss for a new pair, he was berated so soundly his spirit was crushed. He continued going to work, but after a few days his shame outweighed his ten-rupiah salary and he resigned.

The future was dark but at least now he was free from the crushing weight of shame. Still, he had no illusions: there would be difficult times ahead. Nonetheless, Kusno firmly believed that God is the compassionate and the merciful.

One day Kusno's head began to ache. He knew this would pass, supposing that he could get some food, some real food. For two days he had had nothing to eat but leaves. He had thought momentarily about trading his former 1001 shorts for a meal fit for human consumption, but he soon decided against it. Once the shorts were gone the hunger would come back again, probably more acutely. And then how would he cover himself? He also considered stealing, but God forbade him to do so. Though Kusno might never have seen God, his family had for generations feared God's wrath.

Thus Kusno neither sold his rags nor stole; he lived on leaves. His ache continued to ache but he didn't die. Miserably he lived but with a sense of pride.

There's not much more to say about Kusno's 1001 drill shorts. One day they would finally disappear, just as Kusno would one day disappear from the face of this earth. Who knows. Kusno and his shorts might even disappear together.

Whatever the case, Kusno did not renounce hope entirely. He was born into misery, and lived a life of misery. And even though his 1001 shorts might have changed into a wash rag, Kusno would continue to fight against misery, if only to obtain another pair of thick drill 1001 brand shorts, made in Italy.

The only thing that Kusno could not understand was why there was always war. He felt like he was being forced to play the victim.

TRANSLATED BY GEORGE I. BEGLEY

From Kota to Harmoni

THE TRAM WAS PACKED WITH PEOPLE, baskets, empty and filled containers, goats and chickens. The day was hot, and the people and animals were soaked with sweat. The tram stank from sweat and *terasi*. The window ledges were speckled with the tomato-red stains of betel juice.

Breathing was difficult in the tram, but people smoked just the same — to overcome the stink of sweat and shrimp paste. A young woman, a Eurasian, took out her handkerchief, small as a *lemper* wrapping leaf, and put it to her nose. "Who on earth brought that *terasi* on the tram," she complained, "You'd think they would know better. This is first class, after all."

A Chinese man, fat as Churchill, retorted angrily: "Oh, shut up. It's 'co-prosperity' time now, not just for the Dutch." He then bent over and took a small packet from his vegetable basket. "Here's the *terasi*!" he said, shoving the packet towards the woman. "Now what are you going to do about it?"

An old woman, stooped and thin, whose blouse was so full of holes that it looked like a lace bedspread, was being berated by the conductor: "This is first class. What are you doing here? Move to the back! If you don't, you'll have to pay the extra."

"But it's too crowded back there," the old woman begged, "There's no room for me, sir."

"If you don't move you'll have to pay the extra," the driver insisted.

The old woman retreated slowly to second-class. Looking back at the conductor she muttered angrily, "Look at the airs he puts on! He gets a little power from the Japs and this is the way he acts! With an old woman, he acts tough. But you can bet if I were Japanese, he'd be bowing and scraping. Well, piss on him!"

A muscular man, who was wearing no shirt, stood up. "Shut up and sit down!" he snapped.

The tram came to a halt at a tram stop. Outside the people crowded around. "Disembarking passengers, get out, first!" the ticket seller began to scream. "Come on, hurry it up!"

For a brief moment, the people inside could breathe, but a second later the tram was packed again. And then, from outside, came the strident voice of a Japanese: "Let me through, you idiots!"

The crowd jammed closer together to make way for the Japanese.

A younger man looked at the Japanese and frowned: "It doesn't matter if you're first or second class. They still treat you just the same — like animals!"

But when the Japanese came to stand next to him he suddenly had no more to say and looked away. When the Japanese put his arm up to hold on to the leather strap attached to the ceiling of the tram, from his short-sleeved shirt there came the distinct smell of shrimp paste. The young man took out his handkerchief and covered his nose.

Midway down the line the tram suddenly stopped. Perplexed, the passengers thought for sure the tram had broken down or there had been an accident. Everyone looked out and there they saw, in the middle of the tracks, three Japanese holding up the tram. Afraid of losing his own head, it seemed, the tram driver had stopped the tram.

The three Japanese boarded the train, scratching the passengers' arms and hands with the hilts of their sword as they pushed their way in. Once inside they released a laugh of victory.

The tram started off again, squeaking like a rusty pulley. On the curves the people swung to the side. A young woman landed on a young man's lap. As if it happened all the time, the young man hugged the woman around her waist and hoisted her to her feet — but he didn't give up his seat.

By this time the smell of sweat had become intolerable and everyone had begun to complain.

"Makes one remember the old days. . ." said an Indonesian man in a finely-made shirt who, every so often, would brush the dust from his shirtsleeves.

No one responded to the man's comment; it seems his words were commonplace.

At the next stop, a young man and woman got on. Their faces were red from the heat but they laughed and gabbled in Dutch. "Hmm, it's really nice in here," the young man said, "just like in a chicken coop!"

"Still, it's better than walking," the woman said as she took her handkerchief and clapped it over her hooked nose.

"What time is it?" the man asked.

The woman raised her left arm to look at her watch. She tried pushing up the sleeve of her *kebaya,* but it wouldn't move. When she looked again, her watch was sticking out from a hole in the sleeve. "It's 1:30," she said, embarrassed.

The conductor walked through the coach. "Tickets, any more tickets?" he called while passing by the old woman in second class.

The woman watched the conductor pass and when his back was to her she stretched the side of her mouth to the right. "Look at that monkey," she muttered.

The other passengers found themselves staring in surprise at the woman's mouth.

At the Harmoni Building the tram stopped again. From Kota Station to Harmoni, it had taken twenty minutes.

An Indonesian man wearing Javanese headdress and English-made shoes looked angrily at his watch. "It used to take only fourteen minutes!" His voice was shrill, like the rustle of old coconut palm leaves. "Everything's gone to hell these days."

"Why don't you get rid of those people on the running board," he complained to the ticket seller. "Aren't there any rules any more. You should tell them that it's forbidden, that they'll fall off."

The ticket seller stared at the man in astonishment, then contemptuously turned his back on him and blew his whistle.

"Wait!" a number of passengers yelled, "We want to get off."

The tram, which had already begun to move, suddenly stopped and the shoving started again. People were still trying to get off.

The man in the headdress and English shoes grabbed the ticket seller by the shirt. "What are you doing?" he screamed. "Do you do whatever comes into your head? Look before you start blowing your whistle."

The ticket collector grew more astonished. "Who does he think he is?" he mumbled under his breath. He turned away again, but this time not contemptuously. Who knows? Maybe the man was a member of the legislature.

The tram started again. There weren't so many passengers now and only a few remained standing in the aisle. In first class, there wasn't a single Japanese.

A fat woman, who was short like a Japanese, wiped the sweat from her neck. "If I didn't have to, I wouldn't ride the tram at all," she grumbled. "But they took my car, and still haven't paid for it. Why don't they just admit that they're thieves. At least that would be more honest."

"Who took your car?" the man who was seated next to the woman inquired.

"Who else?"

The man laughed in understanding. "Be patient. The great day will come." The words came as easily as sweat drops on skin.

"What? 'Be patient,' you say? If I weren't patient, I would have been in the nut house a long time ago. . ." The woman paused momentarily, then sighed, "Times are hard. It was hard in the twenties, too, but not like now."

A man in dirty shorts leaned towards the woman and whispered, "Better not to talk like that or you might be sorry later."

Near Pasar Baru the tram stopped in front of the theater. More people got on and off. Several people began to climb in through the window. One was a Japanese in civilian clothes.

One of the passengers yelled at the man, "What are you doing? Climbing in through the window like that! Haven't you any manners?"

The Japanese stuttered a few words in broken Indonesian. The Indonesian turned scarlet, suddenly realizing that the man he'd just yelled at was Japanese. But now, being humiliated in front of the other passengers, he plucked up the courage to continue: "That's no way to get in. You shouldn't climb in through the window."

The Japanese man kept on climbing in and once inside the tram, he roared at the Indonesian, "Where do you work? How dare you tell a Japanese what he can't do."

Though inside, the Indonesian man's heart had shriveled to the size of a Japanese cloth after washing, he still didn't want to give in. "And you, sir, where do you work?" he asked. "I work at the Ministry of Interior."

They argued, but the Japanese refrained from laying a hand on his opponent. Standing not far away was a military policeman.

The policeman than said a few words in Japanese to the Japanese civilian. His words seemed sharp and angry. He then turned to the Indonesian and said ingratiatingly, "I've reprimanded him. After all, he was in the wrong."

The Indonesian felt immensely pleased for having won a glorious victory.

TRANSLATED BY THOMAS JOHN HUDAK

The New Java

PEOPLE HAVE NO TEARS left and all they can do now is sigh or complain about the difficulty of trying to get by. Three rupiah for a liter of rice and twenty-five cents for a measly packet of *gado-gado*! Everywhere, people are talking about rice and how tough life is. And they're laying the blame for it squarely on Japan.

Java was famous for its rice, so why is there a shortage? Such a thing has never happened before.

And the Japanese are as bad as the Dutch, out to strip you bare. Or worse, because they do it with a smile on their faces! But no one listens to such comments anymore. Now they're just tired phrases.

On the city streets, outside of restaurants, no matter where you look, you can see half-naked people practically at death's door. They're begging for food, human food, though they'd do justice to dog food too if it came to that. Everyday you see another body lying in the street with a crowd gathered 'round. And if someone in the crowd asks, "What's he doing there?" the likely answer is "Looking for something to eat!"

Seated beneath a tree is a young man with no more clothes on him than on the day he was born — no different from a horse or some other kind of animal. When people pass he tries to cover himself but what can he do with just two hands? Girls look at him and start to titter, as if there's something humorous about the sight.

But he doesn't leave his place; he doesn't even beg — somehow he's managed to retain a sense of shame. All he does is sit there, beneath the tree, not moving until darkness falls. Only then does he move. He keeps his eye on the river and when catching sight of a chicken carcass or a human corpse drifting past, he scurries to the water's edge, pulls the body to the bank, and eats it!

No doubt this young man will also die soon — not from malnutrition, but from gorging himself on rotten flesh.

The whores, too, are dying of hunger in droves; there's that little profit to be made from the trade. Thousands of young women are ready to prostitute themselves, to do anything for money, anything to buy rice for their families. And there are thousands of men who feed on these women. But in the end the girls die anyway. Once a girl loses her bloom there are no honey bees around.

And the young men, even those who still have shirts on their back, are not far from danger. They're wasted from jacking off, as a means of trying to stave their hunger! They, too, will die soon. "From masturbating too much," the doctors say.

The papers are full of news from the front but never mention the effect of the war at home. You'd never guess from reading them what is happening in Jakarta and elsewhere. Reporters are sent out every day to gather news but then all they write about is prosperity for all.

Rice is hard to come by. The official ration is a fifth of a liter per day. But the Japanese are allotted five liters a day, with the surplus ending up in the hands of their maids and house boys. The maids are a prosperous lot, but they pay for their wealth through their womanhood. And when their Japanese employers tire of them they, too, die of hunger.

The Jawa Hokokai organized a large meeting during which the Japanese themselves asked questions to which those present were obliged to answer. For all the world it was like a huge classroom. Are the Government's commands being carried out to the letter? Is the harvest being reaped exactly as instructed? That's what they supposedly wanted to know.

People pondered the questions but none of the speakers provided answers, as if the questions were posers indeed.

People talked about the difficulties of the common man. "There's got to be a change up top," they suggested. "The people in charge don't have the foggiest idea of how things are for the likes for us."

"And how the hell can they," others whispered, "when their bellies are swollen from gorging themselves with rice!"

On the second day of the meeting, the Japanese threw more questions at their captive audience. And then, at the end of this dialogue of the deaf, they advised their listeners that only matters relating to what had been asked about previously would be discussed — as if opinions aired the day before had been for nothing at all.

In Malang, the government-run pawn brokerage pays a phenomenal sum of four rupiah for gunny sacks. The government needs sacks for shipping rice to Japan. Meanwhile, the common folk need them to cover their bodies.

In Jakarta, coffee is short, but in Bantam people are drowning in the stuff. Not that they too aren't dying of hunger — after all, man cannot live on coffee alone.

The streets of Bandung are packed with Eurasian women — all selling their bodies.

Life is hard everywhere. People grumble, but no one has the guts to open their mouths. A government representative, following his return from a circuit of Java, tabled a report of his findings.

Night after night the radio announces that while things might be tough, nobody is complaining. A stiff upper lip, it seems, is the order of the day, and this, the radio blares, is a sign of the people's indomitable spirit! At the end of the speech we learn how impressed the Japanese government is by the whole-hearted commitment of the people of Java.

Tokyo is far to the north, a long ways from Java, but when the call comes down for rice, distance proves to be no object. Up there a telegraph operator turns on his set and, what do you know, two days later the rice is in Tokyo, brought there by planes used for both transport and kamikaze attacks.

Every morning down in Jakarta's Noordwijk district, you see street urchins returning home from church. Their faces are pale and their bodies as thin as stick-figures from lack of proper nutrition.

People have to sell things on the black market, in flagrant breach of government orders, in order to make ends meet. Even the Japanese make use of the black market, but they have their own ways of making money on the sly: the government orders the people to turn in all their ironmongery. In the end the stuff falls into the hands of Japanese civilians who then flog it back to the government at sky-high rates. They can trade without any expenditure of their own.

Life is hard in Jakarta, Surabaya, Plered, all over Java. The people raise their hands to the sky, imploring heaven, beseeching the Almighty for His grace. But each year the paddy ripens, and rice is harvested. . . .Is it God who's at fault?

TRANSLATED BY D.W. ROSKIES

Sanyo

BENEATH THE RADIO LOUDSPEAKER that had been rigged up in the village square sat Kadir, a fried-peanut vendor, whose basket was full of hot peanuts but whose pockets were empty. Over his head an oil-lamp flickered, like a beacon far out to sea. The air that night was so hot it was difficult to breathe. There were no takers for his peanuts that night; the ice-cream man was drawing the potential buyers instead.

Kadir had been sitting there, like some sort of watchman, for the past two hours, itching for someone to talk to. But it was the loudspeaker that blared at him, calling out for people to work as *sanyo*. Kadir had no idea of what was being said. It was like the radio were a foreigner, a squat, yellow-skinned, bloodthirsty up-country tribesman from somewhere outside of Java whose language he could not understand.

Only with great effort did he manage to get his tongue round a few of the words that were spoken. "*Sanyo, sanyo. . .*" he repeated. What on earth did "*sanyo*" mean? "*San*" meant "three" in Japanese, didn't it?

"What's the use anyway," he finally said after considering the matter. "There's no sense brooding just because no one's buying. To hell with *sanyo*, whatever it is. I'm willing to bet that's the reason why business is so bad."

A popsicle vendor, with tattered trousers and a wide-brimmed peasant's hat on his head, then came up to him. The man was shirtless, and his body appeared to be half light and half dark.

Kadir looked the man over. "That guy's popsickles are going to taste even better once his customers get a good look at him," he thought cynically.

Because the popsickle man was no mind reader, he wasn't to know what might be running through Kadir's head, and smiled at Kadir. "I'd like some peanuts, two cents' worth," he said to him.

"You can't get anything for two cents, not nowadays," Kadir answered, contemptuously. "And I'll wager you that *sanyo* is the reason why."

"Be a sport," the vendor begged. "Just a few, anything to dull the hunger. Popsicles are all I've had to eat."

Kadir began to feel sorry for the man. He rifled through his peanuts, found a few small ones, and handed them over. In return the popsickle man gave Kadir two filthy banknotes.

The man popped the nuts into his maw, one at a time. "What's with all these empty ones?" he remarked with irritation.

"What do you mean, 'all these empty ones'?" Kadir retorted. "I only gave you four."

"Where are you from?" the popsickle man then asked.

"From Bogor. I get back there about once a month. I'm a *kumico*, a headman. The Japanese appointed me."

This brought Kadir's interlocutor up short. He was scared to death of the *kumico* in his neighborhood and always played it safe by giving his *kumico* a free popsickle every day. He feared that if he didn't he'd be docked his daily ration of rice.

He now spoke in a soft, respectful, tone: "Then who takes your place when you're in Jakarta, Mr Kumico sir, if you don't mind my asking?"

Kadir colored to hear himself addressed so formally. "My son,

Binu," he replied with pride. "He's just finished school. He's the one with the brains in the family. Me, I can't even read or write. It's when I hear that cigarettes are being distributed in Bogor that I go back, not otherwise. Not to flog them at black market rates, mind you. You won't catch me selling them under the counter."

"Mr Kumico sir, you don't suppose that I could become a *kumico* too, do you?"

Kadir scrunched up his face. "Couldn't say really. It used to be a cinch, but it's harder now." He spoke in a voice reminiscent of Saiko Sikikan, the Java Occupation Force of the Imperial Japanese Army. "Still, it seems I heard on the radio earlier that they're taking on new ones. But you can bet it'll be harder to get in."

"Mr Kumico, sir. This '*sanyo*', what's it mean anyway?"

"Search me. These days people like to use complicated words for the most trivial things."

A customer approached. The man's hair was in a tangle and he was wearing nothing but a pyjama top and boxer shorts. His legs, sticking out from the shorts, were no bigger than rice stalks. "Three cents' worth," he announced.

The popsickle man took out three sticks and gave them to him.

"Not popsickles!" he said crossly, "Peanuts is what I want!"

"But the only thing you can get for three cents," Kadir remarked slowly, "is those popsickles."

"You give me peanuts, or else," the man insisted. "There's more *sanyo* than ever these days, or haven't you heard? If you don't give me those peanuts I'll report you!"

Kadir began to tremble with fear. He picked out a a few small peanuts and gave them to the man, then plucked up the courage to ask: "Please sir, this '*sanyo*' they're talking about. . . What's it mean exactly, if you don't mind my asking?"

"An Indonesian bigshot," the man replied while cracking open a peanut. He then cracked open another but found it empty. "A guy whose head is totally empty, like this!" He flung the shell at Kadir and angrily stomped away.

Kadir turned to the popsickle man. "That does it. We got to find out what a *sanyo* is. Who knows, he could be anything, a scalper for instance."

The popsickle man sighed while looking at his body. "It's a hard life these days. We're like popsicles, getting smaller all the time. In the end all that's left is water and the wooden sticks to be thrown away."

"I see it somewhat differently," Kadir's added. "If you ask me, we're same as popsickles, being bitten into and sucked on by people."

"Well, you know the saying, 'There's more than one path leading to the mosque.' You choose your own poison."

Music was playing on the radio in the square. A Japanese song, Kadir at first suspected, but somewhere in the middle he heard the phrase "my soul."

Kadir applauded when the song came to an end. "That was nice. Sounds like an modern *keroncong* song to me."

The two men were suddenly startled by the presence of another man standing before them. "A penny's worth of peanuts," the man said.

Quick as a wink Kadir reached over for a sheet of paper and wrapped the nuts before giving them to his customer. "Mind if I ask you something, sir?"

"Ask away!"

"What I'd like to know, sir, is if this *sanyo* that everyone is talking about is a black marketeer?"

The customer was both startled and angry. "What did you say? How dare you insult Greater Japan! Do you know who I am? You must be a spy. Come along with me. It's off to the police station with you!"

TRANSLATED BY D.W. ROSKIES

Heiho

KARTONO WAS HARD AT WORK, bent over, in a plausible imitation of a Japanese, his midriff pressing against the desk. He was an office clerk. His work was tedious. And his salary? It seemed that he would never get a rise in pay. He'd been at the job for three years now, and there wasn't a day that went by when he wasn't there plugging away. But had his dedication ever been acknowledged by his superiors? Dream on.

That was why a few months back he'd put his name down as a *heiho,* a recruit of the Japanese Occupation Force. He'd even gone through a physical examination. Whenever anyone asked him why he would say that he was keen to do his share to defend the Fatherland.

Kartono looked up to see the postman making his rounds. He was coming his way! And what great surprise he felt when he opened the letter that was handed to him: his application to join the Heiho had been accepted! He was to present himself at the Heiho barracks that very day.

Kartono was over the moon. Friends offered their congratulations, for all the world as if he were a bridegroom. But even as he beamed with joy he kept repeating his wife's name, over and over again: "Miarti, Miarti, Miarti. . ." And as he spoke her name, his brow furrowed. He scratched his head as if searching for lice.

"You're a hard worker," Kartono's boss said to him, "And I believe that you'll be even more useful for our country as a *heiho*. Wait here a moment. . . There's something I want to give you. Here it is: a testimonial for your diligence."

Kartono knitted his brow once more. "Thank you, sir," he said, "but I'd be ever so grateful if you could write it in Japanese."

Now this boss of his was no nationalist. He was your ordinary chap, a man for whom such things as food on the table for his family and money in the bank came first. As he'd once put it, he always kept to the straight and narrow, with no risk. Risk was not for him. But when hearing Kartono's request he all but hit the roof. "If it's a letter written in Japanese you're after, why the hell are you working here? What do you expect me to do? Bust a gut to learn Japanese on top of everything else, just to write a testimonial letter for you? Brain-fever, that's what you patriotic chaps are suffering from! Tropical malaria, I shouldn't wonder. You're living in cuckoo-land, Kartono. I don't know why I even bother losing my temper with your sort. A bunch of apes, that's what you are, only good for pulling the wool over people's eyes. You see your friends finding a cushy berth thanks to some testimonial or other written in Japanese, and what do you do? You want one too! Monkey see, monkey do. I can't speak a word of Japanese, Kartono, but just supposing I did, supposing I were to write in that chicken-scrawl of theirs that you were a pig's ass, now would you be any the wiser. Tell me that!"

Kartono replied softly: "There's no need to be angry, sir. The idea wasn't for you to do it yourself. After all, there's Supadi here who's just finished an advance course in Japanese."

The boss was finding it hard to get a grip of himself. "Look here, Kartono, I don't give a flying shit about Japanese, no matter how high level it is. You want a testimonial letter? Fine! But it's going to be in Indonesian, one hundred percent! And if you don't like it you can leave. You're not a *heiho* yet, Kartono, and I'm not afraid of you!"

Kartono maintained a steady voice. "Please don't lose your temper, sir. I was only asking, that's all. I'll be perfectly happy with a letter written in Indonesian."

AT THE BARRACKS Kartono was given a uniform and told to wear it in place of the clothes he had come with.

Looking at his new set of clothes, he asked one of the *heiho*, "Excuse me, but don't we get any underwear?"

"I asked that too," the man said, "but the Japanese officer said there wasn't any need. He said that as *heiho* everything has to be done fast. And then he made the sound of gushing water and laughed. That is why, I'm afraid, we get no underwear!"

Kartono joined in the laughter but when he donned his uniform his lower parts started to itch, as if tiny ants were crawling into every pore.

"It feels like that at first," the *heiho* advised him, "but you'll get used to it. You'll even get used to the smell of sweat around here. Now, you go on home, kiss the wife and kiddies good-bye and see that you're back here by eight o'clock."

Kartono hadn't taken two steps before he knew that his shoes were a tight fit. And as he walked one of his heels began to blister forcing him to hobble, with one leg straight and the other dragging along behind.

"LOOK AT THAT *HEIHO*," said a passerby, pointing out Kartono to his son. "You've got to hand it to the Japanese. They certainly know what they're doing when they recruit those yokels. This one here doesn't even know how to wear shoes!"

"But how can they, Dad" the boy asked, "when their feet are so wide from trampling in the fields?"

"It's a sight for sore eyes," the father observed. "Back when the Dutch were running the place it was the educated types that got all the attention. Nowadays, under the Japanese, it's the country bumpkins who matter. Oh they're a clever lot, the Japanese. Country folk are much easier to get fired up."

As if anxious to qualify his observation, the man continued: "Yes, indeed, the Japanese are every bit as clever as the Dutch. It's six of one and one half dozen of another, when you come down to it. It's like Bung Karno says. What was that? You know, 'divide and conquer, vida dan pera.' At least I think that's how it goes."

"You're always using big words in foreign languages," the son commented. "What Bung Karno said just the other day, you can't remember today. It's funny, isn't it, how we tend to forget the things we don't like. That awful woman, for instance. What was her name?"

The father went red in the face. Mortified, he stroked his mop of a mustache. "You shouldn't speak to me like that! You may be a big boy but I'm still your father and you should show some respect. Don't even talk to me about that woman. In all my life I've had dealings with her on no more than three occasions, and then on account of your mother being such a shrew. I'm just warning you not to talk about this at home."

"Take it easy, Dad. All I was getting at is that we tend to forget about the things we don't like, and in no time at all."

"That's not true either. What about your mother? How come I've never forgotten her name?"

The son spoke plaintively: "All I'm saying is why use a difficult word when there's another, easier, word for it? If the Dutch are bastards, say they're bastards. The Japanese are bastards and the Indonesians. . ."

"Are stupid," the father said with a cough. "I've got to hand it to you. You are a clever lad. The best way is the easy way. After all, the meaning is the same!"

WHEN KARTONO ARRIVED HOME his wife Miarti gave him a

sour look and turned away. "Look at me, Ti!" Kartono pleaded.

His wife was livid. "Look at what? At that monkey suit you're wearing? You think I fancy you becoming a *heiho*? I'd rather be dead! What happens if you get killed? Who's going to bring you back to me? The Japanese?"

His wife's anger came as a shock to Kartono. He honestly had thought she'd be tickled pink. "But Miarti, you see, don't you, that I want to do my share for the Fatherland?"

"Your share for the Fatherland? Where's this Fatherland of yours? Tell me that! Have you any idea whatsoever what the word *heiho* means? You nincompoop! A house-boy, that's what it means!"

"But don't you understand? It's you I was thinking of, not myself! Our country's issued an appeal to all her sons. You've got it all wrong, you've got to realize the times we're living in!"

"I don't give a damn about the times. But if you think I'm going to let you join the Heiho, well you can think again! You got a choice: you can throw that monkey suit of yours into the dustbin, or you can give me a divorce and do as you bloody well please."

"But Miarti. . ."

Kartono sighed and wrinkled his brow. For a long time he said nothing. Finally, he blurted out, like a child confessing to some wrongdoing, "Right you are, Miarti. I can't very well go, can I, if you're having none of it. Still, what's done is done, Miarti. Fact is, if I'm not back in barracks by eight sharp they'll have my head on a plate. Anyway, I thought you'd be proud. That's why I kept it secret from you."

Tears rolled down Miarti's cheeks. Pity for her husband filled her heart. "If what's done is done," she said slowly, "how can I say no? Go on then, off with you."

Her words came as a surprise. Kartono was even a wee bit disappointed. He'd thought she'd balk to the bitter end.

"I see now that you don't love me," he said heavily, "otherwise you wouldn't let me go."

At eight sharp Kartono was back in barracks. And eight months later he was dead in Burma. At that time Miarti was four months pregnant, by her second husband.

TRANSLATED BY D.W. ROSKIES

His Balance Recovered

NIGHTTIME AND THE LAND was covered by water. The leaves on the trees bent in the wind, like people in prayer. Lightning was followed by thunder. In Malang the rain was pouring down. The streets were deserted of passersby. Occasionally, a car would go rushing past. Houses were bolted shut. From the radio in the town square came the strains of the song "Lullaby."

Asmadiputra was still at his desk, absorbed in reading *Struggle!*. The newspaper contained an article that had grabbed his attention. National independence was an event six month's old and the city of Malang was planning a lavish celebration.

As he read, his thoughts winged their way back to Jakarta. Life there under the Japanese had been an enviable affair. He had headed a Japanese concern. Not only was his salary considerable; his wife, too, was the frequent recipient of Japanese largesse.

Not surprisingly, then, Asmadiputra had been taken aback by the news of the Japanese surrender. Japan's collapse could be registered in his own sunken features. It meant going back to being a small fry again.

That was another reason Indonesian independence didn't make him jump for joy. Independence would be a serious obstacle to his self-enrichment. He knew full well that in a free Indonesia the whole business of currying favor would be gone with the wind.

Thereafter, every proclamation, every official action on the part of the Indonesian Republic had come in for his mockery and been held up for vilifying analysis. To like-minded friends he analyzed them in a rational, scientific fashion and was able to demonstrate, to both his own and his friends' satisfaction, that the Indonesian Republic simply hadn't a leg to stand on.

At his office he fell to squabbling with *pemuda*, members of the independence-minded youth organizations. In short, he didn't at all care for the idea of power passing from the Japanese to the Republic. Nor did he much care for the flag of Indonesia flying on top of the building.

It was when the *pemuda* began to get tough with him that he really began to balk. Everything they did he saw in an unrelievedly black terms. They stirred in him a desire for revenge. He wanted revenge on the Republic and, also, on Bung Karno, the so-called Indonesian president.

When the Dutch forces landed they brought with them their intelligence services. Their espionage setup had more than just eyes; it had a nose, too, that could sniff its way into every corner. This is how Asmadiputra first came to establish contact with them and how he had been recruited to their cause.

Even though he worked for the Dutch he still had to wrestle with a small voice inside: "You are an Indonesian," it said. "You can't betray your own people." But then a harsher, louder, voice would tell him that he had been humiliated, and by people of his own kind no less. This was why he had succeeded in convincing himself that the Indonesian government was nothing more than a puppet created by Japan, that Sukarno — Bung Karno — was a tool of the Japanese.

The two voices vied with each other until, finally, the harsher voice gained the upper hand. He told the Dutch, "Give me fifty rupiah and I am at your service."

After his decision was made Asmadiputra finally felt some relief. With all the money he now made, he could buy all sorts of things for his lovely wife. Circumstances allowing, he could even take another wife. But this time it would be a woman from the *kampung*, one less educated and more traditional, a childhood playmate of his.

Dutch military action intensified and, in this, Asmadiputra played an important role. He passed on reports to the Dutch about all the movements of the Republican forces that reached his ears. About the activities of the Indonesian *pemuda* he gave especially detailed information. He hadn't forgotten the young nationalists who had worked in his former place of employment. As a consequence of his reports, the *pemuda* were kidnapped and tortured by the Dutch.

And now, even though he had achieved his ambitions, Asmadiputra had yet to feel at peace with himself. He'd taken a new wife and notwithstanding that he was physically contented, spiritual contentment remained beyond his grasp. Often he'd wake from deep sleep, feeling as if someone had been throttling him. It would be difficult for him to breathe easy again, and the soles of his feet would be numb for some time afterwards.

At first, he didn't pay much attention, but its daily recurrence made him decide to seek a doctor's advice.

After the doctor had finished examining him, he went on to ask about matters of a more personal nature. Asmadiputra revealed to him how he'd loved his first wife very much but had recently taken a second one.

The doctor smiled broadly. Asmadiputra supposed that he would prescribed a course of medication. But no. Still smiling, the doctor said, "Go back to your first wife, sir, and live with her as you used to." He took the doctor's advice and went back to live with his first wife. Their life together reverted to its earlier undisturbed state.

But his illness had yet to be cured. True, his hands and feet were no longer stiff. But he'd still rise every night from the pit of slumber feeling as if someone were trying to strangle him. Every night he'd wake crying out for help. Finally, there came a time when he felt quite unable to breathe, that he was literally at death's door.

Unable to stand it any longer, he paid another visit to the doctor. Again the doctor asked him for personal details. And again Asmadiputra gave them to him.

The doctor thought for a moment before asking another question: "Are you sure you're not holding something back from me?"

Asmadiputra struggled inwardly for a long time. He weighed the pros and cons of revealing his dark secret to the doctor. Was it worth it? Could he risk telling that he was working for the Netherlands Indies Civil Administration, and that as a NICA agent he had betrayed both his country and his people?

Not up to the job, he finally answered, "I'm sorry, Doctor, but that there's nothing more I can tell you about myself."

"Well, then," the doctor said as he shrugged his shoulders and shook his head, "if that's all you've got to say, I'm afraid there's nothing I can do for you. Your disease isn't the kind that can be cured by medication. I have just one piece of advice left for you: take yourself off to someplace cool and see that you get some proper rest."

Which is how Asmadiputra ended up in Malang. But it wasn't as if he'd arrived there empty-handed. As well as carrying with him hundreds of rupiah, he had also been lumbered by NICA with the job of finding people who might be willing to work for the Dutch.

In Malang Asmadiputra threw himself into his work and met many new friends from a range of different nations and ethnic groups.

After he had established himself, he began to look for a position that might offer particular advantages to himself. He joined a *pemuda* association. He contributed articles to magazines and newspapers about "The Social Revolution" and "Nation Building." Soon he found himself serving on a government board as a person of some responsibility.

As time went by his name became known. To his friends in Jakarta, NICA agents like himself, Asmadiputra wrote, "Everything's going swimmingly here in Malang."

It was while penning this sentence he felt that there was one thing, at the personal level, that was not running smoothly, and that was the state of his health. Far from having cleared up, the ailment that afflicted him was getting worse with every passing day. Whereas previously he would wake no more than once a night to feel someone's hands at his throat, now it was at least twice a night this happened. Sometimes even three times.

There was something else which threw his heart into confusion: he saw the Republic go from strength to strength with each passing day. Never, not in all his born days, did he imagine that the Indonesian Republic could stay afloat for so long a time. It had lasted almost six months!

The newspaper now lay spread out before him on the table. Six months of Indonesian independence was to be commemorated, with all the stops pulled out.

The longer it rained, the heavier the downpour, but silence surrounded him. Asmadiputra grew dizzy thinking of a thousand and one things about himself and his quandary.

His eyes were heavy but now, more than at any time previously, he was terrified of falling asleep. He was afraid of waking in the middle of the night to find himself being choked to death.

Suddenly he stopped thinking. It was hard to breath. His face grew pale and sweat began to cascade down his cheeks. The torments of the grave, the fires of hell, appeared before his eyes. This flames were all-enveloping. Asmadiputra's shuddered from head to toe. Suddenly he cried out, flung open the door to the house and ran out. He dashed out of the courtyard, and straight to the police station. There all was revealed.

That very night Asmadiputra and his accomplices were detained in prison.

The rain had let up a bit. In a dank police cell Asmadiputra slept like a log. He did not wake up, nor did he feel anybody trying to strangle him. The pressure, the weight on his soul, was off. Thank God.

TRANSLATED BY D.W. ROSKIES

Another Road to Rome

OPEN WAS AT FIRST A PRIMARY SCHOOL TEACHER, after that an Islamic teacher, then a writer, and finally a tailor. Regarding the man's physical appearance, there is little to say: he had two legs, two arms, two ears, two eyes, and one nose. He had two nostrils, too, but that's only natural. In short, Open was like other men, not otherwise. As for his name, however, there is a story there. That can't be denied. What with the thousands of other names — Abdullah, Effendi, Al'aut, Binuwak, and so on — that sound nice and look pretty when written down, the more sensitive reader will no doubt feel cheated if not told how Open got his name.

Obviously Open himself had no part in his choice of name. He was just a baby at the time, a newborn. When he cried his mother would rush to him, her bosom bare, to thrust a protruding nipple into his mouth. He'd stop his screaming, suckle contentedly, and then fall asleep. His concern was not his name. No, the duty of name-giving falls to parents, and anyone who has ever been through the process will confess it's not an easy task.

At first, Open's parents considered asking the local wise man what name would be best for the child. But they quickly discarded that idea for the man was a *dukun* and in Dutch-language primary school they had learned that *dukun* were charlatans, best avoided if one valued ones safety and security. They also considered naming their son "Ali" but they had a neighbor who was named Ali and he was scoundrel, a gambler, and a cock-fighter. They certainly didn't want their child to end up a scoundrel, a gambler or a cock fighter.

Then one night Open's father had a dream. His dream was about New York City and its towering skyscrapers but during the dream, for some reason, he kept hearing repeated, over and over again, the Dutch word "*openhartig*." When bathing the next morning he was still hearing the word; it was as if someone were shouting in his ear: *openhartig-openhartig-openhartig*. Even in the toilet, about which no one is ever *openhartig*, he kept hearing a whisper in his ear: *openhartig-openhartig-openhartig*.

When he related all this to his wife, she jumped for joy. "You fool, that was God's voice you heard. It means that our boy must be *openhartig*, honest and straightforward. We shall call him Open."

The father blinked his eyes. "What are you saying? Name the child 'Open'? Are you crazy?"

As usual in such matters, it is the wife who must, and always does, prevail. And so it was that Open came to be named Open. Whether or not he really did grow up to be a straightforward, *openhartig* man was something that others would determine, but when his mother told him the story behind his name, Open decided that from then on he'd do his best to fulfill her wish: he would be straightforward.

IN TIME OPEN BECAME A SCHOOL TEACHER and every time he entered the classroom he remembered his mother's wish for him, that is to be straightforward. So it was not out of the ordinary when one day he started the arithmetic lesson by saying, "Good morning, children. Yesterday I married a girl from around here but I didn't invite you because I knew that you'd have nothing to give us. But, what can one expect from children? So, tell me, Amat, what is forty-one times forty-one?" Or another time when he told his students at great length about an argument he had with his wife, how he had been wearing only underpants at the time and that because his wife had been holding a *golok* knife in her hands, he had been forced to run away. On this occasion Open had even attempted to reenact the scene for the class. All the children had laughed, of course, though one of them did say, "The teacher is scared of his wife." And another replied, "The poor man, nagged by his wife all the time."

Students of the first opinion were more numerous than those of the second, which is why, from then on, Open was dubbed by his students "Mr Golok". And because *golok*, the word for knife, rhymes with *goblok*, the word for fool, he was soon being called Mr Goblok, too. Whenever he came into the classroom there would always be some wiseacre, shouting at the top of his lungs, "Good morning, Mr Goblok" or "How do you do, Mr Fool?" In the end he couldn't even ride his ancient bicycle through the school yard in the morning without hearing voices calling at him from every direction: "Hey, Mr Goblok!" and "Where are you going, Mr Fool?".

To be sure even the most patient man can get angry and, because Open had always been a person who followed his impulses, when one day his heart told him to grab one of his young taunters and hit him, that is just what he did. He thought his blow had been gentle but apparently it was hard enough to draw blood from the child's ear. The next thing he knew the child's parents were at the school, he was being yelled at by the principal, and, to finish the story, was summarily dismissed.

Before leaving the school, Open confronted the principal: "At the very least, you must admit one thing, and that is," he said quite firmly, "I am no fool. All I did was to tell the kids that my wife had chased me with a *golok* and from then on, for some reason, they started calling me Mr Goblok."

Having spoken his mind, he then left, head bowed. But no sooner had he stepped onto the main road than the raucous cry was heard, now louder than ever before: "Good-bye Mr Goblok, So long, Mr Fool."

Open didn't look back. That's the way he was. Once he decided on a course, he never turned back. He climbed on his ancient bicycle and slowly headed for home.

AT THIS POINT it wouldn't do to leave out the story of how Open came to own his bicycle. No, he didn't steal it; he bought it with his own savings, bought it fair and square. Supposing that he *had* stolen it, he would have said so to anyone who cared to hear. Thus, since he never said a word, there can be no doubt he purchased the bicycle with his own sweat.

What Open did say about his acquisition was thus: he had wanted to buy a bicycle for a long time, and one day a fat Dutch man came to him with a bike saying that he wanted to sell it and asked Open if he would like to buy it. Open thought a moment, then answered that he would but that his savings amounted to only one hundred rupiah. Would the Dutch gentleman sell his bicycle for that price? The Dutch man said one hundred rupiah was enough if he didn't include the two pedals. Open said that was all right and handed over the money. The next day he picked up a nearly naked bicycle. But it worked, which was all Open really cared about. And he was grateful to the Dutch man for blessing him with a bicycle.

Now, in Open's present situation — jobless, chased from the school like an unwanted dog — he felt even more grateful for owning a bicycle. Riding his bicycle, he felt as if he were riding a much loved horse; it was his steady companion in difficult times. He knew, however, that he could sell the bicycle if need be. And knowing that, he felt relieved. He could now turn his attention to other matters.

He thought about what had happened: the students had misbehaved and he had hit one of them, causing the child's ear to bleed. But while he was fired and the children were allowed to go on happily studying at school. Where was the justice in that?

Then he remembered his mother's words: "Open, you must be straightforward in everything. It is in that way you can improve this deceitful world." He decided that his mother's counsel was one hundred percent true. Everywhere he looked he saw lies and well-concealed corruption.

The schoolroom, as Open saw it, was the best place to plant the seeds of straightforwardness. That is why he had become a teacher in the first place. But, in the end, that is also why he had been dismissed. Suddenly, for the first time in his life, it occurred to Open that the world was filled with ingratitude. He thought of how Jesus Christ had been crucified and the prophet Mohammad had been harassed and attacked.

Thinking of the prophet Mohammed, Open became overcome with an irrepressible desire to renounce the world, to trade his trousers and hat for prayer clothes, the *sarong* and *peci.* He immediately steered his bicycle to a bookstore where he bought Mohammad Yunus' translation of the Koran.

So began Open's life as a Muslim. But there were numerous difficulties to be overcome before he could achieve his new goal. The first was his wife who was very upset by the news Open brought home that day. But then, for a wife, what does the loss of her husband's job mean? It means no more comforts, no more fire in the kitchen, and shame before one's neighbors.

The argument that followed between Open and his wife was incredible, but would have been of no consequence if only his wife hadn't asked, "Why did they call you Mr Goblok in the first place?"

Faithful to the promise he had once made to his mother, Open told all. When his wife heard that her name had been paraded before the class, she could restrain herself no longer. She snatched the translation of the Koran from Open's hand, tore it to pieces, and threw it into the fire.

Well, when fighting reaches the point of burning one another person's treasured possessions, from then on every road back to resolution is closed, and there's only way out — divorce.

Seething with anger Open left his wife and headed for the used-goods dealers to sell his bicycle. The bike had cost him one hundred rupiah; now he couldn't get more than thirty-five. One dealer said that all he wanted was the frame; after all the tires were bald, the pedals were gone, there was no carrying rack, and the wheels were rusted. Another dealer was interested only in the wheels because the frame was bent, the tires were bald, and everything else was missing. Yet another said that all he really wanted were the pedals, but when he saw that they were gone he changed his mind and bought the spokes instead. In the end Open sold the bicycle for thirty-five rupiah and with the money went home to his parents' village.

OPEN'S VILLAGE WAS LIKE OTHER VILLAGES — no lights, no bookstore, no out house. When Open's bowels gave him trouble he went and squatted on a dike; while fiddling with a rice straw, out came everything that troubled him. But one day, while fiddling with a rice straw, a village girl came upon him. Open was so embarrassed that he ran all the way home with his stomach still in knots. Once home, he stamped his foot and shouted at his mother, "We have to have an out house. I can't stand it. Surtiah passed by and made me feel embarrassed."

Open's mother agreed to his request. "Poor Open," she thought, "he's just divorced his wife — I'll do whatever he asks, so he'll be happy and can quickly forget his sad past."

That's the way it is with mothers, always giving their children love, always concerned for their welfare. But with Open there wasn't in fact any need for his mother to worry. Once he had his thirty-five rupiah, he no longer remembered the past — not his wife whom he'd just divorced, not the principal who had abused him, not even the bicycle that now belonged to the junk-dealer and was still in his mind's eye.

But that was Open: He quickly forgot the past and never thought about the future. He was a man of the moment. As time moved ahead, he moved with it. If time were to stop, well, Open would long since have departed this world.

No, Open's thoughts were not as his mother supposed. He had merely been embarrassed by Surtiah, nothing more. That's the only reason he had pressed his mother to build an out house.

But might there have been another reason? In fact there was, but since Open himself hadn't breathed a word about it, nothing could be certain. Yet one had to ask wasn't there something suspicious in the way Open had run home with his stomach still aching. Wasn't it odd that Open he had pressed his mother for the out house? Wasn't it strange that he had been embarrassed by Surtiah about something no one in the village would ever feel ashamed about?

Surtiah was a village girl, born and bred. Her toes were splayed and her palms were rough — not because of mosquito bites but from the bite of a hoe-handle. In one way only was she like a city girl — she had large breasts. But the reason for this was different. When city girls have large breasts it's because of dancing and fun but Surtiah's breasts were large because she had healthy blood, because she was active every day: hoeing and harvesting rice and carrying meals to her parents when they were out working in the fields.

Maybe she didn't have a pretty face but that's not important when love is about to bloom. That is, if we can call Open's feelings towards her "love."

Open himself had already forgotten about his meeting with Surtiah. He spent his time deep in thought, his mind off in another world. "What is the purpose of life on earth?" he asked himself. Was it straightforwardness as his mother had said? "Yes," he answered. Then should he go back to being a teacher and spreading the seeds of straight-forwardness to students? "No," he said to himself.

"What is the goal of religion?" he wondered. "Holiness," he answered. But how was holiness achieved? "Through truth," he discovered. But how could one find truth? "By being straight-forward," he decided. How could he best spread this knowledge to others? "By becoming a religious teacher," he finally answered.

Thereafter Open buried his face in religious books. He soon learned the twenty attributes of Allah by heart. Every day he read *Surat Yassin*, the prayer for the dying. He performed the five daily prayers without fail, and soon became known in the village as the young *mualim* newly arrived from the city.

No one becomes great overnight. One must begin at the beginning. Then slowly, step by step, one becomes known and establishes oneself as a great philosopher, a great writer, a great prophet, or even a great *mualim*.

Open was aware of this. And thus, with a reluctant heart, he forced himself to begin all over again as a teacher — though this time as a teacher of religion, teaching children the Arabic alphabet. But what had happened before now happened again: he found himself face to face with a classroom of impudent children.

During the first months there were no incidents. The children roared their ABCs like cars roaring down a highway at sixty kilometers per hour and soon Open was able to set aside the primer to start the task of instructing his pupils in the foundations of Islam.

One of the foundations of Islam is the twenty attributes, that is the twenty unquestionable attributes of Allah. These a student must swallow whole, without any proof such as Spinoza might offer. Like quinine tablets, they might be bitter to the taste but provide hope for recovery.

As with all Islamic studies in the village or at the neighborhood prayer house, the twenty attributes are learned by rote; the pupils must chant the attributes, one after the other — *ujud, qidam, baqa*. . . existence, preexistence, everlasting, and so on — until the twentieth is reached.

Unfortunately for Open, one of his pupils was Javanese and, like all full-blooded Javanese, had difficulty pronouncing the letter "a" at the end of a word; the boy simply could not stop himself from saying "o." Thus, when chanting the twenty attributes, he began, "*Ujud, qidam, baqo,*" at which point Open was forced to stop the child and say, "It's not *'baqo'*, but *'baqa.'* Aa, Aa, Aa. . ." The boy began to chant again, "*Ujud, qidam, baqo. . . Ujud, qidam, baqo. . .*"

One of the other students, irritated that the lesson was being held up so long, waited for a chance to vent his annoyance. When the Javanese boy began the chant yet again, his angry classmate extolled, "*Ujud, qidam,* bacco, cigars, cigarettes. . ." Hearing this, the rest of the class burst into laughter. Several other students chimed in, repeating the whole series: "*Ujud, qidam,* bacco, cigars, cigarettes. . ."

Open's face became red with anger and he hit the impudent child. Fortunately, this did not bring about an early end to Open's career as a religious teacher but it did make him sad.

At home Open told his mother about what had happened and while at first she tried to comfort him it then occurred to her it should no longer be her responsibility to comfort her son. "Indeed," she mused cheerfully, "he needs the comfort of a wife. . ."

Without even thinking, she said to her son, "You should marry again. You need someone to express your feelings to. I'm an old woman and sometimes don't understand you. How about if I ask Surtiah?"

On hearing the name Surtiah, Open remembered their first meeting, when he was squatting on the dike emptying his stomach while fiddling with a rice straw. He remembered how embarrassed he had been when he ran home clutching his belt. He still blushed at the thought.

"I'd be embarrassed," Open told his mother.

His mother failed to grasp the direction of Open's thoughts. "What's there to be embarrassed of?" she asked. "Our family is better off than hers. And you're a *mualim*. Surtiah is just an ordinary village girl. Let me speak with her parents."

With fairy-tale speed two weeks later Surtiah was Open's bride, and when he first smelled her sweet breath, he knew his mother had made the right choice.

One day Open took Surtiah to the city where they met another *mualim*. The odd thing about this religious teacher was he didn't wear a *sarong*; he wore trousers like a clerk in an office. He didn't wear a prayer cap either. Instead his hair was smeared with 4711 and was combed like a college student's. At first Open was disappointed, and Surtiah even more so, but when the city *mualim* began to speak of religion, truth and the purpose of life, both Surtiah and Open knew that clothes were not the true measure of a teacher's wisdom and greatness.

"Many people have the wrong idea," the city *mualim* explained. "Take clothes, for example — people think a *mualim* shouldn't wear trousers. But nowhere in the Koran or in any other religious text is there a single line forbidding the wearing of trousers. I wear them on purpose to combat this general view. People also say a *mualim* shouldn't write, which is why I also write."

"You write?" Open asked. The truth is, he asked not because he was surprised but because, during the past few days, he himself had been considering doing the very same thing. There was so much he wanted to say to so many people. A classroom could hold only thirty, maybe forty, pupils. At the very most, he might have seventy villagers studying with him. But by writing it is possible to speak to thousands. "What is it that you write?"

"Everything, even novels," the city *mualim* answered.

"Novels?" Open was surprised.

"Yes," the *mualim* answered. "A love story between a girl and a boy, for instance. The usual thing, but with content. . .with content."

AFTER THEIR CONVERSATION with the city *mualim*, Open and Surtiah returned home. Not too long afterwards there came to the village a troop of short, yellow-skinned, and slant-eyed men, all dressed in khakis and high boots and carrying weapons of death.

Poverty soon became widespread. Open's *mualim* clothes were in tatters and he had neither money nor cloth for new ones. Finally, when Open's sarong was nothing but a rag, Surtiah said to him one night, "You have lots of trousers. Why not wear them? Don't you remember what the *mualim* in the city said?"

Open hugged his dear wife and the next day, and the day after, and every other day, he wore trousers. The villagers were dumbfounded. Some of them whispered, "Look, the teacher has gone mad." Others dared to say, "The teacher must be a Japanese spy. Be careful! Don't go near his house. And don't let the children study with him any more."

In the end this situation became intolerable, especially for Surtiah, and she suggested to her husband one night, "Let's go to the city. There you can try to write. Remember the *mualim* in the city."

Open hugged his dear wife and they left for the city. Open was going to become a writer.

The first person they went to visit after their arrival in the city was their friend the trouser-wearing *mualim*. Open had intended to chat with him about his work as a writer in hopes of learning something helpful. But unfortunately he wasn't home. His wife told them that he had been arrested several months earlier by the Japanese for refusing to cooperate with their request to read sermons prepared by the Japanese Bureau of Religious Affairs.

Upon hearing this news, Open's perspective on everything suddenly changed. When he saw someone in the street wearing trousers made from gunny-sack cloth he asked himself "Why?" When he ran into a beggar on the street he didn't immediately think "Idler!" or "Animal!"; instead he asked himself "Why?" When he saw corpses on the banks of the Ciliwung River he also asked "Why?" And when seeing people walk past the corpses, barely noticing their presence, he asked himself "Why, oh, why?"

He thought about the *mualim* who had been arrested by the Japanese and when he again asked himself "Why?" everything suddenly became clear as day. The Japanese hadn't come to bring prosperity. They were here to trample religious freedom and to starve and strip the Indonesian people bare. And what did the Indonesian people do? They slept, slept just as they had for the last three centuries. The words shot from his mouth like a torpedo from a submarine: "The people of Indonesia must be awakened! Awakened! Awakened!"

At nearly the same moment Open saw his mother's face and heard her say to him, "Open, you must be straightforward."

From then on Open became another man. Or rather he was no longer a man, but the boiler of an overheated locomotive ready to explode, to pulverize everything in its path, ready to free the human race of its depravity.

Seated behind his desk with a blank piece of paper, Open saw the somnolent Indonesian people planting castor-oil trees and in the sky above them, airplanes whose engines were lubricated with the same castor oil, dropping bombs on the people planting trees.

He envisioned peasants stooped over as they harvested rice and heard the words of Multatuli, author of *Max Havelaar*, resound in his ears: "*De rijst is niet voor dengenen, die zij geplant hebben. . .* The rice is not for those who plant it. . ."

He also saw sights that were now a daily occurrence such as

naked men, on the banks of the Ciliwung, fighting over the corpse of a dog that had been carried downstream by the current.

Open wrote on his paper, "Corpses fight over corpses. . ."

Open stared more intently. "The man who had been lucky enough to grab the corpse of the dog was now eating it."

He wrote down, "Corpses eat corpses. . ."

He watched the others as they stared enviously at their friend as he ate the corpse of the dog alone. The man eating showed no sign of wanting to share his spoils. All sense of humanitarianism was gone, as was any feeling of shame.

Open wrote on his sheet of paper, "Dogs eat dogs. . ."

After the man had finished eating, he leaned against a shady tree. He slowly closed his eyes, then rolled over on the ground dead, his hands clutching his belly.

Open wrote, "Corpses become corpses. . ."

The man's companions cheered. Pedestrians passed by smoking Kooa cigarettes.

Open wrote, "Sleep-walkers smoke Kooa cigarettes."

Then, Open saw his mother saying to him again, "You must be straightforward in everything you do."

Open began to write frantically, his hand unable to keep up with his thoughts. He wrote and wrote until he had completed his composition.

Manuscript in hand, Open went to an editor. The man was small and thin. To Open the man's face said "hedonism" and his clothing "Japanese money." Nonetheless, he appeared to show true concern for Open when he told him, "This composition could be dangerous for you. You should hide it — or burn it. Why write about cow shit when you have the beauty of nature before your eyes. Look at the Priangan Mountains or at the Selekta area near Malang and surely your outlook on life will change. Surely then you will laugh and be happy. Life is not as bad as you have pictured it."

Open left the editor's office with rancor in his heart. He grumbled to himself about the man, "The way he looks, the clothes he wears... It all fits!"

At home, Open thought about the editor's words. "Cow shit — that what he'd said I write. Well, he's right. It is cow shit. It does look bad, but if it's spread around like fertilizer it can make trees grow. The trees are the Indonesian people who are now fast asleep."

Open wrote another composition and hid it among Surtiah's pieces of wrap-around *kain*.

He soon came to know the joy of writing, but one day Surtiah said to him, "Your stories are very good, but we're nearly starving to death. You must find yourself a job."

At first Open responded kindly to the suggestion, but after a while his answers to her suggestion grew sharp. Finally, one day, when Open was busy writing and Surtiah was pressing him to look for work, Open threw down his pen and shouted, "You're always pestering me. You think I don't work? Get out. Go back to the village."

Open meant what he said and Surtiah felt that it might be best for her to go. Hopefully the day would come when he would need her again and she could return to the city. But for now, she had better go home to the village. Sadly Surtiah returned to her parents' house.

Open felt relieved to be free of his wife. He continued to write — every day another short story. It made no difference to him that they weren't published; he knew he must listen to his heart and his mother's advice. If to do that he must leave his wife, that didn't matter. She could be dead as far as he was concerned.

Only one of Open's stories was published. When the Japanese Cultural Center sponsored a contest for the writing of legendary tales Open submitted an entry. The legend he wrote was one he had once heard and had always wanted to write down. The tale was about a Papuan man who lived one hundred years ago. Like all Papuans this man worshipped an idol but the idol never brought him fortune. His luck at fishing was always poor. Dozens of times he had bowed before the idol, but his catch remained as small as ever. The man finally concluded that worshipping the idol was useless. Why prostrate yourself before a god who cannot help you.

The man left his village and traveled to the seashore. There he met men such as he'd never before seen. Their bodies were covered with cloth; they did not go 'round naked like him. But what puzzled him most was the great number of fish they caught. One day he plucked up his courage and asked them, "Who gives you so many fish?" The men all pointed to the sky and answered in unison, "Allah, The Lord God."

The man's curiosity was piqued and he began to study about this god who gave these men so many fish. Eventually he embraced Islam when he became convinced that it was only Allah, The Glorious and Exalted Lord, who had the power to determine human fate.

Open's story was published and even received first prize but later the Japanese censor regretted that he had let the story through. Too late he had realized that the story was dangerous, that it was a veiled attack on the Japanese emperor. Yes, it was too late, but not too late to arrest Open.

Open was called into the headquarters of the Kenpeitai, the Japanese military police where, instead of being politely questioned, he was immediately beaten and forced to confess that the story was an attack on the emperor.

The fact is there would have been no need for violence. Even without having been beaten first, Open would have told them, in his straightforward way, that indeed had been the purpose of his tale. But he also told them he hadn't just made the story up; he had heard it himself and thought that it might be true.

After his confession, Open was beaten again. Blood covered his whole body. He was made to bathe in cold water until he was stiff and then to sit out under the hot sun. After several days the wounds on his body had healed of themselves. It seems that was the Japanese way of treating wounds: wash them until stiff, sun them until baked, and they'll heal themselves. There was no need for iodoform, tincture of iodine or salve. Nature alone provided the cure. It was almost beyond belief.

After that Open was locked in a cell. His body became thinner and thinner. But fortunately he wasn't beaten any more.

In his cell, Open realized for the first time the value of freedom. There are two types of freedom: bodily freedom and spiritual freedom. Bodily freedom can be taken away — as was happening to Open. But no one could take away his spiritual freedom. Though his body was surrounded on four sides by high walls, his thoughts were free to go anywhere. But was freedom the purpose of life? No. Freedom was only a means to achieve that purpose. What was the actual purpose?

Other people might have a different answer but for Open, who had been educated in a Moslem society, and who had once become a *mualim,* there could be only one answer. The purpose of life is to honor Allah's commandments in order to go to heaven and there be united with Allah.

At times he thought of his mother: "You must be straightforward in everything you do."

Open now knew that his mother was in fact saying the same thing. God. . . Purity. . . Straightforwardness. . . Truth. To be sure, his mother was not just a simple village woman. She had attended Dutch primary school in the city. But because she associated with simple people, she expressed things simply too. She might say "straight-forwardness" instead of "God" or "purity" or "truth" but in fact she meant the same thing.

Since becoming a writer, Open had read many books on philosophy. Locked up in the military prison, eating, drinking, defecating, and urinating, all in the same tiny cell, at times made Open almost mad with despair. When his suffering was at its worst he found there was only one philosopher to speak to of his misery. That was Boethius. And at time he felt as if he himself were Boethius, imprisoned for trying to do good to his fellow men, imprisoned by the good itself.

Boethius had said that misery itself is nothing. It is man's skewed attitude towards misery that leads them to despair and makes them feel themselves to be victims of fate.

Boethius' words were etched in Open's heart as truth and were a comfort to him once he became convinced that his mission in prison was to overcome his mistaken attitude toward suffering. Suffering was not the enemy, the enemy was his attitude. When he had freed himself of this attitude and saw his suffering for what it truly was, he gave thanks to God and thanks as well to Boethius.

That is how Open was able to endure his misery in the Kenpeitai prison. When the Republic of Indonesia was proclaimed and he was released, it's true that his body had grown thin, but inside he had grown fat with thought. This was no longer the same Open. This was an altogether different Open — more aware and able to view life from a broader perspective. That's why during the Revolution he didn't go along with the killing of Japanese, Eurasians, and Chinese. Revolution is good, he felt, but if it began to produce evil side effects then it must be immediately checked and channeled towards a better course, towards the realization of its ideals. Revolution is good. He himself had experienced a tremendous revolution in himself. Revolution is simply the consequence of a natural evolution, a slow and orderly process. But revolution is not killing. Revolution means shaking people from their dreams, rousing the sleepers, and making a long leap towards the realization of ideals.

Meanwhile, Open's manuscripts came to be published and his name came to be known far and wide. Once or twice he received letters from readers threatening him if he dared to go on writing his filthy stories. Other readers called him a fool, but these were the exceptions. For the most part he won praise from all sides.

Open enjoyed rereading his stories, but something inside him told him that he could never write stories like that again. If he were to write again his output would be very different — more refined perhaps and more weighty in tone. But for the time being he couldn't write anything at all. He had wrestled hard with the complexities of life, with its purpose: truth, purity, and what his mother called straight-forwardness. But he sensed the presence of a certain emptiness inside himself, one that could only be filled with a philosophical succulence that comes only from a firmer world view.

No. For the time being he would not write. He would release his earlier manuscripts one at a time and not try to write anything new. He was certain that one day the void inside him would be filled and at that point he would be able to write with renewed conviction.

WHEN THE REVOLUTION BEGAN TO SUBSIDE, Open was forced to look for work. His first job was as an assistant to a tailor, but soon he learned to sew for himself.

Open's work brought him into contact with the dregs of every nation: English, Dutch, Nepalese, and even native or *Inlander* soldiers. Every day he came in contact with all the forms of evil there are in the world, if only as a bystander. If he were the same person he had once been he would have transformed his views into short stories and novels. But now all he did was watch, silently record what he saw, analyze it and mold it into a philosophical outlook that might fill the void in his heart.

At night, before he slept, he was haunted by images. He saw a Nepalese soldier killing a woman, robbing her of both her jewelry and her honor, buying cloth with the woman's money, and ordering him to sew a shirt from it. Then a Dutch soldier stood before him speaking of nothing but bringing security to Indonesia and saying that he had never troubled anyone, indeed he himself wouldn't harm a fly. There was also an English soldier who cheerfully boasted of having just come from Bekasi where he had burned a village to the ground. His image was replaced by that of a native soldier but it was not a human figure that stood before Open. A human being is an individual whereas this man bore not a trace of individuality. After begging his captain for new clothes, he then begged Open to lower his price for sewing them. When Open refused, the soldier threatened him with a bayonet. Open remained calm and let himself be shot.

At this point Open would laughed and say to himself, "Evil people might retain the physical characteristics of mankind, but in their hearts they are wild beasts."

Thus it was that every night Open learned something new and he became certain that each of the lessons he learned would lead him towards true straight-forwardness, and not the straight-forwardness he had practiced as a primary school teacher.

Little by little, as the emptiness inside him was filled, his former desire to be alone and his egotism diminished.

Why had he sent Surtiah home? Because he didn't want his thinking disturbed with the problems involved in looking for a job. That he now knew was the essence of selfishness. He no longer felt that way. On the contrary, each day he grew more convinced that Surtiah was essential to his spiritual life. She would no longer be a distraction for him; she was his backbone.

Open immediately wrote her a letter. Three days later she arrived with her father and mother. Open's mother came along too. At once Open's house was changed into a hive of activity and Open no longer had the time to think about the things that had preoccupied him for so long. But that didn't annoy him. He felt that a change of this kind was necessary, at least for a time. And when the old people went back to their village, he felt that he was parting with people whom he loved dearly and who loved him.

Surtiah noticed the dramatic change in her husband and was now happier than she had ever been before.

TRANSLATED BY MARK CAMMACK

Why I Didn't Set Up My Own Business

I AM AN EMPLOYEE of an Indonesian import-export company. My office is a newly painted garage. I have a desk the size of a pocket handkerchief and an aged rocking chair.

When I come to the office in the morning, I open an almost-empty cabinet and take out a stack of last month's newspapers and put them on my desk. These are the acts of a man eager to start in on heaps of accumulated work. After this, I sit on my rocking chair and read the papers until my head droops onto my chest.

One time, while asleep in that chair, I found myself dreaming. The Chief Executive Officer of the company came to me and asked in a nasal voice: "Why aren't you working?"

"Why do I have to work?" was my reply.

"You're my employee, aren't you?"

"No," I asserted, "I'm an angel."

Hearing this, he opened his wallet and gave me five hundred rupiah. "Go back to being an ordinary human being," he told me, then jumped into his sedan.

After two months of being treated like an angel — a being that doesn't need to eat or drink — I was, one Sunday, invited to the CEO's home.

His house was beautiful and modern and located on one of the city's main streets. The grounds were so large that the CEO was able, or perhaps considered it necessary, to have separate entrance and exit gates for his car and the cars of cabinet ministers. He had mentioned to me one or two times that he was certain ministers of state would call on him at home.

Because I came on foot, I didn't have to worry about which was the entrance and which the exit to get to the house.

I was given a warm welcome by the CEO and two other people. One was a pretty woman who turned out to be the CEO's new wife, and the other, a middle-aged man, who was the vice president of a small bank.

After inviting me to sit down on a comfortable chair, the CEO spoke to his guests: "All of you probably know about the new import regulations, that we now have to pay forty percent in advance before we can import anything. I ask you, gentlemen, where are we supposed to get that kind of cash? You can be sure that no one is going to want to use his own savings for such a purpose."

Because the CEO was looking at me as he spoke, I felt obliged to offer my opinion. "But these regulations don't apply to our company. . ."

I would have continued but the CEO's face turned red with anger causing me to immediately look down at my shoes.

His next words seemed to be a reprimand: "How can they not apply to our enterprise? We are an import-export company, aren't we?" He laid special stress on the word "import."

After that, the CEO did not look in my direction again. Instead, he directed his remarks to the vice president of the little bank and, in the course of their conversation, an agreement was reached that the bank's president would use his influence with a credit bank to obtain a loan for the CEO. For his assistance in acquiring the loan, the CEO promised to appoint the bank president director of our import-export company.

Quite unexpectedly the CEO then said to me: "And beginning now, I appoint you deputy director."

The blood drained from my face and it was not until I arrived home I fully realized that I had become a person of very great importance for the national economy.

So it was then that the CEO began coming to the office almost every day. Every time he came he would ask if there were a letter for him, but every time he asked I would have to spread my empty hands and shake my head regretfully.

Until one day, a letter really did come. As the CEO's car stopped in front of the office, I waved the letter at him from inside the office. He jumped out of his car and like a small child snatched the letter from my hand. He paid careful attention to the letter as he opened it and read its contents.

Suddenly, he shouted like a mad man: "We got it! We got it!"

Once he was back inside his car he yelled to me, "Come tomorrow to the house and pick up your pay."

This was the first joy that I felt during my stint as deputy director.

Even though I received only one month's salary — unless he thought that the seven hundred fifty rupiah he gave me was for five months' work — I began to have real hopes for this firm. The CEO had been able to borrow four hundred thousand rupiah, the maximum permitted by the credit bank. Now surely, I thought, the company would move ahead as it ought.

In my imagination I would receive piles of letters each day from both inside the country and abroad. I cheerfully would seek tenders from overseas and gradually form a staff of assistants.

But none of this actually happened. Our import-export company didn't import or export anything at all and the firm's director never stuck his nose inside the door again. Eventually word came that the director was buying up agricultural land and homes. Thus, from being the director of a company, he had become a prominent property holder.

As for me, I went back to being an angel. I had long since thrown away my deputy director's tie and was spending my days doing nothing but playing chess with an unemployed friend of mine.

Unfortunately, since my friend couldn't tell a castle from a knight, he made the same moves with both, so we finally stopped playing that game and just swapped stories all day long.

One day my friend said to me, "You have lots of experience in this company. Why not set up one of your own? I can help you get credit from a bank. If you like, you can become director and I'll be a member of the board. You'll be able to live in comfort and won't have to work here any more."

I clasped my friend's hand in earnest. "That's a great idea. Let's do it! Try to arrange it for me."

In the garage the two of us danced for joy.

The next day my friend returned to inform me that he had called on the Minister of Justice and had explained to him our reasons for setting up a company. The Minister had agreed in principle to help but told my friend that he needed one hundred rupiah to cover various expenses. This one hundred rupiah was to come from me.

Before my friend could finish what he had to say I interrupted him: "It looks like my director found out about our plans to set up a new firm because yesterday he paid me two month's salary all at once."

"Does that mean you won't be setting up our own company?" my friend asked.

"Now there's no more reason to," I explained. "The CEO has promised to pay my salary regularly from now on."

This made my friend angry. "You don't have the guts is all. And to hell with the guy who calls himself a company director but is afraid to compete with us." I didn't respond. I looked at my shoes with their holes in the toes.

But my friend's attitude had changed completely. He was like a man begging. "Well if you really did get two months' pay, then surely you won't mind lending me a hundred rupiah. We're in a real mess at home right now."

With some reluctance, I lent him twenty-five rupiah and in my heart of hearts, I hoped that with twenty-five rupiah as capital he would, with luck, be able to set up a company that was one hundred percent national.

TRANSLATED BY A.L. REBER

A New Parliament in my Home

A NEW PARLIAMENT OPENED one miserable Sunday, but don't get the idea that a new democratic state was established as well. The new parliament opened in no place other than my own house. It was raining that Sunday and my four children were unable to go outside; that's when they suddenly decided to be members of parliament. And so it was, starting then, that I was a very special father, probably without equal in the entire world: all of my children were parliamentarians. But rather than make me happy, the effect was just the opposite because the new parliament, at its very first meeting, immediately initiated discussion of my position as father.

Honorable Member Nirwan, who was thirteen and acted like a dictator during the proceedings, stated that a father must heed the demands of his children and comply with their requests. In failing to do so he would have shirked his responsibilities and must, therefore, be deposed. He mentioned as an example that he had asked me for a moped quite some time ago but not only had I not granted his request, I had not even given him an answer, or so he said.

I was in my study reading when hearing this and so I stopped and listened quietly as the session continued. My heart beat a little faster because if the other three members agreed with Honorable Member Nirwan's finding it would mean that I would have to flee and that they would surely install another father in my stead.

Honorable Member Damayanti, who was twelve, agreed with Honorable Member Nirwan; not just one, but two of her requests had not been fulfilled. Her first request had been for permission to wear lipstick, which my wife had initially granted but which I had subsequently overruled. The second request had been for permission to drink coffee but that, too, I had refused. For my failure to heed her requests, Honorable Member Damayanti found that I had quite clearly neglected my fatherly duty and, therefore, must be deposed. Moreover, she said, these two refusals had made it obvious to the outside world that I was unable to keep up with the times and must therefore be labeled as reactionary and anti-revolutionary.

After hearing Honorable Member Damayanti's words you can understand why my heart beat even faster. I was forced to ask myself whether my children had already agreed to oust me and had established the new parliament only as a democratic facade to justify their actions. Fortunately, the next speaker, Honorable Member Riyadi, who was eleven years of age, disputed the first two speakers' findings and this gave me new hope.

Honorable Member Riyadi suggested that the motion his fellow MPs, Nirwan and Damayanti, had floored and discussed was nothing more than bombast, pure theory that would be difficult to put into practice. "Just ask yourselves, dear Members of Parliament," Honorable Member Riyadi posed, "are you truly proposing that we should seek another father as his replacement? Even supposing that this were theoretically possible, it still leaves the question of whether we have the heart to do such a thing, and more to the point. . ." — these were Honorable Member Riyadi's words — ". . .whether we have the power!"

Honorable Member Rizal, who was ten, quickly came to Honorable Member Riyadi's support, and this caused my hopes to rise even more. To myself I said that Riyadi and Rizal must love me more and promised that if I were not overthrown I would buy them both a popsicle.

At that point Honorable Member Nirwan, who had all the characteristics of a dictator, angrily rebuffed the opinions of MPs Riyadi and Rizal, stating he had once read in a book that in Communist China there was no problem in deposing a father from his position if he were obviously reactionary or anti-revolutionary. Further, he also said, human beings had evolved from animals and because animals did not have sensitive feelings it should not be difficult to part with ones father. "Blood ties are a human construct, completely unnatural!" so said Honorable Member Nirwan.

At that the session dissolved into chaos. MPs Riyadi and Rizal wanted to leave the assembly — They didn't agree with Honorable Member Nirwan's pronouncement — but were prevented from doing so when the latter grabbed hold of their shirts, thereby causing MP Riyadi to throw his fist square into MP Nirwan's eye and starting a fight that went on for several minutes.

Listening to all this in my study I wondered whether to go out and break up the fight. If I didn't, MPs Riyadi and Rizal might also begin to think of me as reactionary and anti-revolutionary for being indifferent to my duties as a father. On the other hand, if I were to break up the fight, Honorable Member Nirwan might take the view that I was siding with Riyadi and Rizal, and the result would be even greater aversion towards me. Damned if I did, damned if I didn't, I decided to let the fight proceed and to wait for the outcome.

Luckily my wife had heard the quarrel, too, and she soon came to break it up. From my room I heard MP Nirwan, the dictatorial revolutionary, sobbing and crying. Subsequently I discovered that Riyadi's first blow had been followed by three others all which had hit their targets — MP Nirwan's eyes and nose.

After the fight Honorable Member Damayanti moved for a five minute recess and then for a vote on their father's position, but

MPs Riyadi and Rizal summarily rejected the motion by running away from Parliament House, the new easy chair I had recently purchased.

Thus the first session of parliament had ended in blows, without a single issue decided and I ensconced in my position as father. But for how long that would remain the case, I could not predict, for parliament could be reconvened at any time to determine my fate. However, because no vote had been taken and MP Nirwan was still sobbing, Honorable Member Damayanti adjourned the session. She then asked Honorable Member Nirwan whether he had a car, and if not, whether he would like to go off with her in her car.

Honorable Member Nirwan replied that he didn't have a moped, much less a car, and gladly accepted Honorable Member Damayanti's offer. By then Honorable Member Nirwan's tears had almost subsided and he asked her where she had got the car.

Honorable Member Damayanti replied that as a member of parliament it wasn't difficult to obtain a car, that numerous foreign companies vie to appoint parliamentarians to their boards of commissioners because of their positions. "We don't need to do a scrap of work," she reported, "and we're given cars as well, as long as we take care to use our influence with other MPs so that they don't make any moves to harm the company."

Honorable Member Damayanti then proceeded to tell MP Nirwan that if he wished to have a car, she was in a position to suggest that he be made a commissioner too. With that, no doubt, the car would come automatically. And supposing that the president of the company didn't want to give him a car, then she, Honorable Member Damayanti, knew what tactics to use: he would keep calling the president, constantly requesting to borrow his car. In the end, when the president grew tired of lending his car, he would give Honorable Member Nirwan a car of his own, quite likely a Fiat 1100, which is what had happened in her case.

Upon hearing this Honorable Member Nirwan stopped crying and began to laugh along with MP Damayanti. Yes, he, too, wanted to be on the board of commissioners. After that the two MPs went off in Honorable Member Damayanti's car, that being a bolster from her bedroom.

And I, who had been following all this from my study, was very happy, not just because I hadn't been ousted from my position, but for the knowledge that, of my four parliamentarian children, two were now to be on the boards of commissioners of large foreign companies. I immediately promised myself that while parliament was in recess I would work on MPs Nirwan and Damayanti, not to make sure that I would not be deposed but rather to ensure that I would be driven around by the two of them in a Fiat 1100.

TRANSLATED BY MARTYN COVE

A Mayor's Downfall

IN THE BUSY MARKET of a small town renowned for its safety, an English lady was stabbed in the back with a knife in broad daylight. Both of the town's newspapers printed the story with large headlines on the front page and for the first time in the history of town's newspapers, both papers sold out.

The first paper came out with a sensational report, revealing proudly — in bold type, no less — that the English lady was considerably older than her husband. As a result the town's police detectives were compelled to draw the conclusion that the husband of the English lady had paid someone to kill his elderly wife.

The other paper, not to be outdone, declared — in bold type as well — that the stabbing of the lady was related to an ongoing wage dispute at the company the lady's husband ran. This led the police detectives to a second possible theory, that the workers' union had paid someone to kill the English lady.

For the two following nights the chief of police went sleepless as he tried to find a way to tie together these two theories. It was on the second night that the link was made. And though it might be hard to believe, it wasn't the police chief himself who made the link, but his wife. How this came to pass no one can be sure because it happened in bed in the middle of the night but, regardless of how the chief's clever wife first discovered the link — to this day it is thought that the idea came from the police chief himself — the combined theory goes as follows: Because the husband of the English lady wanted to free himself from his much older wife, he exploited the anger of his workers, who were upset about their wages, by arranging to have her killed.

Quite understandably, after this hypothesis became publicly known — though no one could say who leaked it — the peaceful little town descended into uproar and confusion.

The leader of the workers' union issued a statement denying that there was any connection between the union and the stabbing of the English lady. Armed with Marxist theory, he declared that the workers' weapon was well known, that the workers' weapon of choice was not the knife, but the power to strike and, if necessary, to strike again.

Throughout this uproar the townsfolk themselves did not remain passive and took to blaming one another. Residents of Neighborhood A, for example, accused residents of Neighborhood B. Residents of Neighborhood B must have been involved, or so the reasoning went; after all, the English lady had been stabbed from a distance and, as everyone knows, people from Neighborhood B are known as expert knife throwers.

To this accusation Neighborhood B replied that Indonesians had never been known as expert knife throwers; therefore the person who stabbed the English lady must have been from England. Robin Hood was famous for throwing knives, was he not, and also an Englishman?

Fortunately the feud between Neighborhood A and Neighborhood B fizzled out soon thereafter when the police announced that the English lady had not been stabbed from a distance but from close proximity. The assailant had disappeared with the knife used in the stabbing. If an expert knife thrower had been involved the knife would have been left sticking in the chest or the neck of his victim.

Meanwhile, at the town hospital, the English lady breathed her last breath, but according to the doctor who had treated her, it was not the stab wound that had finished her off, but the town's potholed roads. From being transported to the hospital over the town's potholed roads, the lady had lost so much blood that nothing could be done to save her.

When the doctor's findings were announced the town's political parties were greatly relieved; now they need not fear a protest from the British consulate. It was not a local person who had killed the English lady, but one of the local roads; therefore the killing could not be said to have been politically motivated. And as far as those potholed roads were concerned, this was a domestic affair in which no British or foreign consulate could involve itself. Nonetheless, as a goodwill gesture, the political parties announced that the first item on the agenda of the upcoming meeting of the town councilors would be the road problem.

And in fact the problem of the town's roads did become the main topic of discussion at the meeting of the Town Council that was held one week after the stabbing. Representatives from Political Party A, an Islamic-based party, declared that leaving the town's roads potholed and muddy was an act of hypocrisy; the roads' condition made it difficult for people to go to the mosque and prayer houses to perform their acts of worship. Spokespeople of Political Party B, a nationalist party, declared that potholed roads were an obstacle to progress and growth of the national economy; as such, the mayor's neglect in this matter represented a major failure and therefore, the representatives demanded, the mayor must resign forthwith. Representatives from Political Party C, the populist party, declared that the party would not object if the mayor were to step down because many of its own party members were more than willing to become the mayor.

And although the mayor declared that he couldn't understand why the stabbing of an English lady had become an issue of potholed roads and why it should affect his position. He also explained that the roads were potholed because of a delay in receiving funds from the Ministry of Finance in Jakarta; because the State Oil Company didn't want to sell its asphalt supplies, another supplier had to be found. And notwithstanding what the parties wanted, the mayor, not being a party member, would remain in his seat, thank you very much.

A week later the political parties announced that they had chosen a new mayor. By chance it was the doctor who had earlier treated the English lady. The person who stabbed the English lady has yet to be apprehended by the police and so is still at large, but the small town that was once peaceful is now peaceful again, and each and every resident of the town looks forward with confidence to the future that no more English ladies will be killed by the roads of their town.

TRANSLATED BY MARTYN COVE

RINI PWI

"to dry the tears from these eyes" — Los Palos, East Timor

Text by Rini PWI and Yudhi Soerjoatmodjo

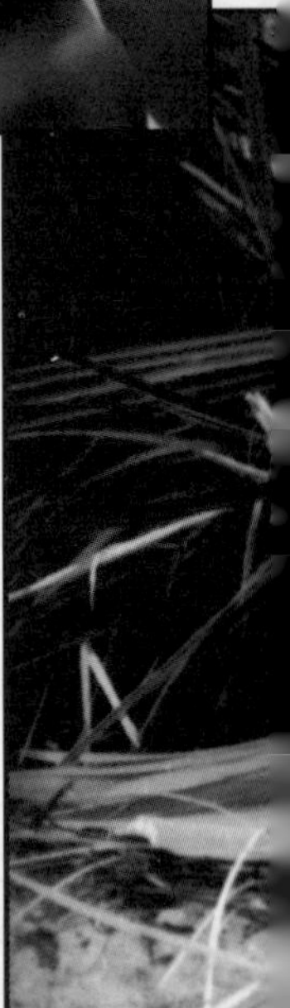

THE ROAD TO LOS PALOS, leading four hundred fifty kilometers to the east of Dili, twists and turns through hills and valleys. Passing Baucau Market, the local gathering place, one enters the heartland of East Timor, where the landscape is spotted with dwellings made from *lontar* leaves.

Although centuries of Portuguese colonization converted the majority of East Timorese to Catholicism, here the attraction of ancient tradition and sacred leaves still remains strong. Almost foreign to the town's two thousand inhabitants is modern technology and they, like their ancestors before them, till their fields with human and animal strength alone.

The population has a fearsome reputation as warriors but their austere diet — with corn as their staple food and meat from tree-dwelling animals such as monkeys and *kuskus* — indicates a more spiritual and melancholic character.

ON THE SIXTH NIGHT after each full moon inhabitants gather to perform *tho,* a purification ritual. Arm in arm, moving in circles, they perform a slow and rhythmic dance. As tears stream down ancient faces from their mouths flow lyrical *sau* that echo in the surrounding forest and fade in distant crashing waves:

ahira sukira haikare,	in the wake of war comes emptiness,
helenu cemu tu' uralahe,	and the desire to do nothing but rise,
eceremu nina vaya haikare	to dry the tears from these eyes. . .

ULIL ABSHAR-ABDALLA

Religious Restrictions

IN 1996 *INDEX ON CENSORSHIP* published an extensive report on liberalism in the Moslem world. According to the report, Western secularism, whose impact today is world-wide, cannot alone undermine religion and that true faith cannot be marginalized or destroyed. In fact, as *Index* states, Western secularism frequently stimulates forceful growth in religiosity, often in the form of fundamentalism.

What, one might ask, is the meaning of the term "liberalism"? While there is no codified interpretation of the term in the Islamic world, in this context "liberalism" refers to an attempt to rationally interpret a religion (read: Islam). But does such a definition suffice? From the point of view of Sunni and Syi'ah Muslims, the rational approach is irrelevant; it is *ijtihad* or legal reasoning that plays the more important role. Why is it that these two orthodox sects are poorly disposed towards liberalism?

Writers on the history of Islamic thought often refer to *mu'tazilah*, an Arabic term whose literal meaning is "people who avoid the mainstream" but, in this context, means those religious philosophers who see reason as the only medium for understanding the Koran. For these people reason holds center stage, outshining even the role of God's message which, in their view, has no meaning for the human race unless it is mediated by reason.

Not surprisingly, according to *mu'tazilah*, the first and most important task of every Moslem is *nazar*, to think. Sunni Muslims, on the other hand, believe that one first must believe. Thus, their respective rule of thumb, would be, for the *mu'tazilah*, think then believe, and for the Sunnis, believe then think. Liberalism is thus, more or less, the former's model of faith, the manner in which they practice the Islamic faith.

Liberal Moslem intellectuals often cite the *mu'tazilah* as justification for liberalism. Liberalism is not, they believe, a new phenomenon, one without precedent. Liberalism is an integral part of the history of Islamic thought and not foreign to it. Certain contemporary Islamic thinkers, the Egyptian philosophers Hassan Hanafi and Zakki Najib Mahmud to name just two, loudly proclaim that it is essential to revive *mu'tazilah* liberalism if creative dialogue is to be brought back into Islamic thought. They suggest that it is the waning of liberalism that accounts for the decline of Islam in modern times. Opponents of liberalism explain the decline of Islam from another angle, namely that the adepts have lost God's message.

Syakib Arsalan, a Moslem intellectual and a pioneer behind the idea of a modern Islamic revival, formulated a dictum that has proved popular: the difference between the Western and Moslem worlds is that the West excelled after leaving their Book (religious doctrine) behind while the Islamic world declined after doing just the same.

Throughout Islamic history, liberal thinkers have generally come from the Philosophical and Sufi traditions. These same people have also been the frequent target of persecution. Suhrawahi the Martyr and Al-Hally, both of whom were Sufis, are two examples.

Riffat Hassan, a noted feminist thinker, traces the origins of liberalism to Sufism and to Islam's philosophical school of thought because, in her view, Sufis and philosophers see God as a source of unlimited truth. God's "truth" is not something that can ever be completely formulated or finalized. Meanwhile, Moslems who subscribe to the juridical view of God believe that all of God's truths are set down in the Koran. As such, in interpreting the Koran human beings need only establish fixed hermeneutic boundaries.

Riffat Hassan also states that the philosophical and Sufi traditions are less popular than "Fiqh," a discipline dealing with Islamic jurisprudence, and that throughout the Islamic world, almost without exception, Fiqh is the sole underpinning of Islam's intellectual tradition. Philosophy and Sufism, when allowed to develop, have been able to do so under Fiqh auspices. As we know, for example, from the polemical treatise by Al-Qhazali, entitled *Tahafutul Falasifah*, it is the ambiguity of philosophers that is widely seen as a reason behind the demise of philosophy in Sunni Islam. In *Ilhad Ar-Raddu Alal Bathimyya*, Al-Ghazali also criticizes the heterodoxy of Sufism. For the guardians of orthodoxy, philosophy and Sufism are a Pandora's Box which questions faith and upsets centuries-old interpretations. Predictably, it is the philosophers and the mystical Sufis who have most often experienced persecution, from the burning of their works to execution.

For the Sunni and the Syiah, Islamic tradition is static and unchanging, and those members of the faith who diverge from, or take a subversive view towards, this tradition risk persecution by their orthodox brethren. Just as if liberalism had never been a part of the Islamic tradition, liberal Moslems are seen as opponents of tradition. The problem here of course is that "tradition" is being defined by the guardians of orthodox Islam who feel that within Islam there is no room for more than one point of view. They do not recognize that every tradition has its contradictions and that in any tradition, Islam included, there are divergent opinions.

The popular or dominant interpretation of a tradition can be traced to sociological factors, for example, to political support by governmental authorities. Such is the case in many Islamic communities where the orthodox domination of the interpretation of faith is directly linked to government authority. In this regard, the parallel between the government's interests and "teleological stability" is well recognized. This shared interest between government authorities and official interpreters of the faith creates a mutual support network for the two. With the increasing popularity of the view that Islam is a monolithic construction, more and more liberalism is seen as something that must be eliminated.

SHARING THE FATE of numerous classical thinkers, today's Islamic liberals find that writing can be a dangerous occupation. Take the case of the liberal Egyptian writer, Nasr Abu Zeid, who had, as one of his long-term projects, the analysis of Koranic texts. It was his book on the subject, *Naqdul Khitabid Diniy*, that eventually led to his damnation.

The basic premise of Abu Zeid's book is that conflict within Islam can be traced to the differences between the ambiguous text *(mutasyabihat)*, one with many possible meanings, and the unambiguous text *(muhkamat)*. Most Islamic thinkers agree on one point, namely that the interpretation of an ambiguous text ought to be based on an unambiguous text. But where is the border between the two? Abu Zeid suggests that "the border" is a political contrivance. And it is here that let us say, a quantum leap took place. This view has a radical implication, namely the construct that is Islam was formed by a historical process. Previously the "Islamic construct" had been seen as meta-historical, from beyond history and located outside of history. The construct, therefore, held absolute truth. Abu Zeid's suggestion that Islamic thought represents a historical process opened a new perspective — because Islamic thought is historical, it is therefore relative. Another radical implication of Abu-Zeid's suggestion is that the Koran is a historical, not a meta-historical, text and therefore represents a "stage" on which conflicts of interpretation took place.

Abu Zeid's views created a stir in Egypt. He was removed from his position as a lecturer at Cairo University and deported to London (whereafter he moved to Leiden to teach). Branded as an unbeliever, he was also pressured to divorce his wife, because under Egyptian law, as an unbeliever he could not have a Moslem wife. He refused to divorce his wife and took her with him, out of the country, to the land of "unbelievers" that offered him protection from religious persecution.

The case of Abu Zeid is one example of the danger that can come from thinking or writing in an orthodox Islamic world. But in a border world such as Indonesia, the danger is no less acute and many of Indonesia's neo-modernist Islamic thinkers — Nurcholis Madjid, Abdurrahman Wahid, Djohan Effendi, and Ahmad Wahib, to name just four — have faced repression for simply expressing their views.

Among Indonesian Islamic liberals today there are three main issues of debate. The first is how to reinterpret Islam in order for it to match the pace of modernity. This issue serves as the core of the Islamic Modernist movement pioneered by Nurcholish Madjid. The second issue involves the interpretation of Islam as a transformative power; those Moslems who believe in Islam's transformative power concern themselves less with modernity per se than with its social and political implications, which they see as marginalizing the less-fortunate. Hence, they often bring to discussion topics that the government deems to be "politically sensitive." The third issue is the historicization of Islamic thought. This phenomenon has been heavily influenced by the post-structuralist movement and has captured the imaginations of many young Moslem intellectuals, with Mohamed Arkoun often-cited as the authority. Moslem intellectuals who deal with the third issue engage themselves more with the text as well as its interpretation.

One of the interesting facets of the liberal Islamic experience today is that it is not taking place among traditional Moslems in the villages, but rather among well-educated Moslems in urban areas. The "Islamic Renewal" movement pioneered by Nurcholish Madjid is but one example. This movement has attracted a great deal of attention among urban Moslem communities. Two reasons are cited for this: first is that Islamic liberalism is an issue that touches the "spiritual need" of the educated. Second is that spiritual security is an important issue in the modern world. Interestingly, "security" seems to be found in the orthodox interpretation of Islam. Hence, the main opponents of Islamic liberalism are the urban educated Moslems who yearn for spiritual "asylum."

Herein we face the paradox of modernity. While Islamic liberalism is partly inspired by modernity, its main opponents are the modern educated Moslems, who have found their spiritual security threatened and have reverted to seeking salvation in traditional religion. The contemporary Islamic tradition has two unique aspects. On the one hand, it emerges from the unsettled conflicts triggered by the free thinkers who continuously question standard or authorized interpretations and who assume that any interpretation is basically historical. This, as shown earlier, is a perennial problem. On the other hand, it emerges from the conflict between liberal thinkers and their opponents, which is fundamentally a manifestation of the internal conflict of urban educated Moslems who are threatened by the facelessness of modern society. The opponents of Islamic liberalism come from two ends: the guards of established tradition, as well as the modern urban Moslems who long for orthodox tradition. Such conditions make writing a dangerous practice for Islamic liberals.

TRANSLATED BY SANDRA HAMID

MELANIE BUDIANTA

Lessons in Scholarship

FOURTEEN YEARS AGO, on my very first day as a lecturer, I arrived in the classroom eager to impart fresh knowledge to my students. What I got, instead, was a lesson in what it meant to be a scholar in Indonesia. I was then teaching an undergraduate course on modern drama, which started with Samuel Beckett's *Waiting for Godot* as an introduction to the absurdist genre. A few days after the first session, a member of a campus religious organization approached me and asked permission to sit in on the next session. Towards the end of class the following week, the guest student stood up, recited some lines from the Koran and the first principle of the national ideology, Pancasila (i.e., "belief in one God Almighty"), and then started lecturing me and the rest of the class on what a good Indonesian citizen should and should not believe in. I was able to steer the discussion that followed towards the question of religious differences and the distinction between normative and academic discourse. To my relief, this seemed to satisfy everybody.

The day ended well, but the experience left me musing. My first brush with academic censorship had not been the result of intervention by the State (whose censors are far too inefficient and unmotivated to concern themselves with the contents of an esoteric course taught by an unknown junior lecturer). Nor had it been imposed on me by my senior lecturers or the dean. Rather, it had come from my students, young people barely in their twenties.

The questions this situation raised — Had the indoctrination of the State Ideology during the course of the students' educational development been completely internalized? Was there less tolerance for religious diffrences among students now than there was before? — were not ones that could be easily answered. But one thing I did become certain of was that heightened sensitivity towards anything that might upset the religious-, ideological-, or ethnic beliefs severely handicaps academic freedom in Indonesia. A lecturer at the Faculty of Psychology was unable to find a publisher for his dissertation on psychological traits of the Minangkabau people; prospective publishers worried that the person's findings might upset members of that influential ethnic group. Results of a research project on the sexual activity of young people in Yogyakarta gave rise to a cry of protest among provincial legislators, and was subsequently banned.

Fear of upsetting public opinion forms the basis for self-censorship, especially since government sanctions often follow on the heels of public uproar. One year ago, a publisher shredded three thousand copies of a book already in print after concluding that the book would bring "bad luck" for the company. This book, which dealt with the topic of presidential succession, featured an introduction by Sri Bintang Pamungkas, a former legislator who was then being tried by the government on charges brought against him for remarks he made in a lecture presented before a professional association in Germany.

Indonesian scholars are forced to work within the constraints of government restrictions The banning of works written by individuals who have been marked as leftist or communist, such as Pramoedya Ananta Toer, severely limit the choice of reading material for students of Indonesian literature. Chinese studies in Indonesia has suffered greatly from a blanket ban on any material containing Chinese characters. Prior to the fall of the communist regime in the U.S.S.R., Indonesian scholars of Russian studies were prevented from using materials available from the Russian Cultural Center. They were also prevented from maintaining contact with persons connected to the Russian Embassy.

Prohibition on the ownership and dissemination of books containing Marxist, Leninist and Communist theories causes numerous problems, especially for scholars hoping to bring books on these subjects into the country from abroad. Several months ago, a scholar wrote in a letters-to-the-editor column that a book he had tried to bring back was confiscated by customs officials simply because the book's title included the word "Marxism." A similar incident occurred at Diponegoro University in Semarang where a low-level official became suspicious of a box of books shipped from the United States.

In spite such incidents, most of which are instigated by petty officials, supervision by the government over the implementation of such restrictive regulations is generally both lax and inconsistent. This gives scholars some leeway in "interpreting" or circumventing the regulations. When Pusat Bahasa, the government-funded National Language Center, embarked on a writing project on Indonesian literary history, the scholars who were invited to sit on the committee made it clear that the project must not exclude banned books, in particular those of Pramoedya Ananta Toer. The fact is some lecturers actually do discuss Pramoedya's works and have students write about them as well. One colleague taught a course entitled "Repression and the Novel: A Psychoanalytic and Marxist Approach" without receiving any kind of reprimand. A recent seminar on the subject of "Multi-culturalism in the United States, Australia and Great Britain," included a discussion of the concept of multi-culturalism in Indonesia. Foreign participants at the seminar asked whether such frankness in the discussion of cultural politics was commonplace.

Unfortunately, in academia, even these little freedoms are illusory and can disappear without a trace should a scholar or lecturer "abuse" his freedom or to allow things to go "too far" by crossing the border of a professional discipline and entering into the realm of politics — as if there is a clear distinction between intellectual and political subjects.

In August 1996, a few weeks after the occurrence of politically-motivated riots in Jakarta, a group of young lecturers at the University of Indonesia discussed a plan to publicly appeal for the more humanitarian treatment of protesters who had been detained by the authorities, some of whom were their own students. Needless to say, this plan did not materialize because most of them started having nightmares about what might happen to themselves even before they had drafted the appeal. In their imaginations, one wrong move meant their careers would be over.

In Indonesia, it is not necessary to label someone a Communist to end his career; even casting suspicion on one's "background" — familial, social or otherwise — might be enough to do the job. And once a person has been targeted there is almost no escape. A post-graduate education at a foreign institution, where one is exposed to extreme liberalism or individualism, is sufficient to make one ideologically impure. Even a person of prominence who happens to say the wrong thing at the wrong time, i.e., namely when there is within earshot an intelligence officer eager to please his supervisor, might be blacklisted for being branded an intellectual nuisance. This random, irrational, and absurd game of chance between intellectual freedom and government restraints is enough to make any thinking person insecure.

In 1977, after a period of student unrest, the government introduced a new academic policy concerned with "Normalization of Campus Life" which was intended to keep students' minds on their studies and their bodies off the streets. The impact of this policy on campus life was not immediately apparent. In 1992, however, ten years after my first teaching assignment and fifteen years after the implementation of the policy, when I returned to Indonesia from my studies abroad, I recalled my first teaching experience and prepared myself for a rigorous round of ideological interrogation on my first day back in the classroom. Instead, what I found was a group of docile-minded students, eager to get through the semester as quickly and safely as possible. When I tried to engage them in discussions on intellectual or cultural matters that lay outside the strict class agenda, I found them unwilling to venture onto possibly unsafe ground.

This is the state of Indonesian academia which is made up of the nation's most educated people. Unfortunately, now it seems that "educated" means little more than passing through twelve years of elementary and secondary rote-learning exercises: memorizing maxims, completing lessons in the basic sciences, memorizing historical, social and literary data, learning State ideologies by heart. In this system there is no room for nurturing love of reading, critical thinking and writing.

After graduation from secondary school, college-bound students choose a discipline in which to specialize and then, entering college, must stick to that discipline. Based on European models, Indonesian universities place emphasis on separate and autonomous "faculties," each with its own specific methodology. In such a compartmentalized system, students rarely take courses outside of their own field and do not engage in academic dialogue with students from different faculties. Students of law and economics, for example, do not take courses in literature. Students of English literature do not study economics and politics.

At the advanced level, and though I may generalize, the rule today for students appears to be to read the minimum number of books required to complete a paper or thesis. Students do not read for the sake of intellectual curiosity or enlightenment. And publishers who specialize in academic textbooks find a steady market for their books, as do publishers selling religious-, how-to-, and light-reading books. General reading materials on social issues and the humanities seem to be viewed as luxury items.

This is the academic environment in which Indonesian scholars must work, read, and write. I was once asked why so few Indonesian intellectuals write full-length books on sustained themes, and publish collections of essays instead. I suspect that the answer to that question is that Indonesia's academic environment is not conducive for serious or long-term engagement with ideas. Scholars and academicians are generally underpaid, overworked, and often times saddled with administrative tasks.

Indonesian intellectuals find themselves undernourished. Libraries with adequate research facilities are practically nonexistent. Researchers, especially in the humanities, are at a disadvantage in competing for grants, most of which are earmarked for the fields of technology and industry. This climate forces Indonesian scholars to be resourceful.

Growth in use of the internet, which has opened new horizons through its easy access to inter-cultural and global dialogue, provides some hope of change in Indonesia's reading and writing environment. But, based on my own classroom experiences in 1982 and 1992, I do have to wonder what surprises the classroom of 2002 will hold.

TRANSLATED BY THE AUTHOR

STANLEY YOSEPH ADIPRASETYO

Political Prohibitions

IN LATE APRIL 1996, the Indonesian public learned, through the media, of a government ban on the ownership and distribution of *Nyanyi Sunyi Seorang Bisu* (*The Mute's Soliloquy*), Pramoedya Ananta Toer's moving memoir about his experiences on Buru Island. The fact that the Attorney General's office had actually banned the book a month earlier, on March 26, prompted questions about the process of book banning in Indonesia. Some people speculated that the government's delayed announcement was simply a ploy to learn the names of sellers of banned books. After all, previous to this time, whenever a book was to be banned the Attorney General would call a press conference and distribute copies of its authorization for the ban to the mass media.

Almost every year, at the Indonesian Book Publishers' Association (IKAPI) book fair, Indonesia's Minister of Education and Culture delivers a speech criticizing the lack of support for the country's book-publishing industry. Another common complaint is that Indonesia's book publishing industry is far behind that of other developing countries, both in terms of the quantity and quality of the books it publishes. Yet another is that book prices are too high, far above the reach of most ordinary Indonesians, that even schoolbooks are too costly as a result of collusion between government officials and publishers.

Problems in Indonesia's book publishing industry have taken a heavy toll on the quality of Indonesia's human resources. The banning of books and the threat of legal action against publishers, distributors, and owners of contraband publications not only limits room for discourse, it also limits opportunities for the acquisition of knowledge. Books are the future. Through books, writers impart their experiences, dreams and accumulated wisdom. Through books, future generations can discover the records of lives and patterns of behavior of those who have come before them.

That said, the Indonesian government would appear to hold some kind of record for book bannings. During the past thirty odd years the government has banned more than two thousand books. The first bannings in that period took place shortly after the government's massive crackdown on the Indonesian Communist Party (PKI) in 1965. In November of that year, the Assistant Minister of Elementary Education and Culture for Technical Education, banned seventy book titles.

This action was followed by the wholesale banning of all books and other written works by eighty-seven writers who had links to, or who were thought to have links to, the PKI, whose influence the government was trying to eradicate from Indonesian soil. Notable here is that none of these eighty-seven writers was ever formally tried for their "crime" though some of them were later arrested and exiled to the Buru Island Penal Complex. Included in this same ban was a supplementary list containing the names of twenty-one authors whose books were to be purged from the Department of Education and Culture's library and archive.

It is estimated that in the wake of the attempted communist coup in September 1965 the government banned more than five hundred books. However, because all of the documentation relating to these books was destroyed it is impossible to ascertain the exact number. Sadly, many of the books were also destroyed — mostly by government authorities but also by frightened citizens who feared possible arrest, exile or even death for the new crime of owning "Communist" books.

In Indonesia today it is not only "Communist" books that are banned. A glance at the list of titles that have been banned over the years reveals an amazing range of topics: books on sex education, science, history, and fiction have also become fodder for the censorship mill.

Materials deemed by the government to be overly explicit in sexual matters include not only magazines like *Playboy* and *Penthouse*, novels by Nick Carter, and the drawings of Valentino; the censors have also targeted art and photographic books, including one entitled *Madam Syuga* that contained sensual portraits of President Soekarno's widow, Ratna Sari Dewi.

Censorship also extends to clippings, magazines, newspapers, bulletins, journals, almanacs, cassette tapes and even unsigned leaflets. In the 1980s, the reason behind the banning of books and cassettes could be traced to their religious content. Keep in mind that at that time that the government was exercising great pressure on all organizations, religious groups included, to adopt the state ideology of Pancasila as their sole ideological basis.

Academic books, historical works in particular, are often deemed unsuitable for public consumption. This list includes Soe Hok Gie's dissertation, entitled *Di Bawah Lentera Merah* (*Under the Red Lantern*); *Tan Malaka*, by the Dutch historian Harry Poeze; *The Military and Politics in Indonesia* by Harold Crouch; *Ersatz Capitalism*, by Yoshihara Kunio; *Sang Pemula* (*The Pioneer*), by Pramoedya Ananta Toer; and *Indonesia: The Rise of Capital* by Richard Robison. Even *Tempo Doeloe* (*Former Times*), a historical anthology of early Indonesian literature was affected, but the primary reason here seems to be that it was compiled by Pramoedya Ananta Toer and published by Hasta Mitra, the publisher with the record for having the most books banned.

Government censors no longer have their home in the Department of Education and Culture or in the Coordinating Agency for the Consolidation of National Stability (BAKORSTANAS); they are to be found in the office of the Attorney General which, under current law, has the sole authority to ban books.

Following its designation as the government's official censor, in March 1989 the office of the Attorney General issued a circular calling for every publisher to submit one copy of each new book to its office. Because most publishers either ignored or were reluctant to fulfill this request, in October of 1989 then Attorney General Sukarton Mamosudjono established a "Clearing House", a team of censors as it were, whose job it is to oversee and evaluate all printed materials. The team comprises representatives from the offices of the Attorney General (from the Division for Intelligence and the Supervision of the Mass Media), BAKORSTANAS, the State Intelligence Coordinating Agency (BAKIN), the Armed Forces Intelligence Agency (BIA), the Department of Information, the Department of Education and Culture, and the Department for Religious Affairs.

This team holds regular meetings to decide on the banning of "sensitive" publications but there are ad hoc meetings as well for the discussion of "urgent" matters. The data this team compiles are used by the Attorney General as the basis to ban works the team deems "capable of disturbing public order."

As to the definition of "capable of disturbing public order," the Attorney General points to any publication that opposes Indonesia's national ideology (i.e., Pancasila), its constitution, laws and social norms, or harbors potential for disrupting the nation's political-, economic-, and social structures. This includes publications that contain or promote Marxist, Leninist, or Communist teachings or concepts; any publication that might undermine social unity or public faith in the nation's leadership; offensive words; immoral pictures; anything promoting obscenity or pornography; anything that insults God or any one of the five religions recognized in Indonesia; anything that might undermine national development; anything that might promote or create divisions between Indonesia's ethnic-, religious-, racial-, and social groups; anything that conflicts with the President's annual report on Broad Outlines of the Nation's Direction (GBHN); and, as the Attorney General appended to the end of this list, "etcetera, etcetera, etcetera" — meaning that the government has, in short, the power to ban virtually anything.

Whenever the Attorney General's office announces another banning, the announcement cites the legal articles on which its decision was based. One of the most frequently cited articles is Government Law No. 4 PNPS/1963, a highly controversial piece of legislation commonly known as the "anti-subversion law." Under this law anyone who helps to distribute or disseminate a banned book automatically serves to undermine the unity of the Republic of Indonesia and therefore, may be tried on charges of subversion. It was this piece of legislation that was invoked in 1989 against members of a study group in Yogyakarta who were arrested and then sentenced to eight years in prison for distributing the novel *Rumah Kaca* (*The Glass House*) by Pramoedya Ananta Toer.

Despite the risks it would appear that banned books, magazines and leaflets are in great demand. One example is the magazine *Independen*, the successor to *Forum Wartawan Independen*, which was banned on March 24, 1995. Published by a group of Indonesian journalists, this magazine has a print run of eight thousand copies, but an estimated readership of nearly three hundred thousand or roughly forty readers per copy.

Because booksellers in Indonesia believe that "critical" publications are likely to be banned they are eager to sell such materials. Thus, by banning a book, the Attorney General tends to boost a writer's sales.

Increased demand for a banned book also raises potential profits for all parties involved. Following the banning of the autobiographical *Memoar Oei Tjoe Tat* (*The Memoirs of Oei Tjoe Tat*), which had been selling at Rp. 15,000 per copy, the market price increased four fold.

In Indonesia the marketing and distribution of banned books has not decreased despite growth in access to the internet. Indeed, it seems that the popularity of banned literature is on the rise. Readership is no longer limited to political activists; banned materials can now be found in taxis, planes, trains, the offices that line Jakarta's main thoroughfares and the humble dwellings of Jakarta's poorer areas. What does this phenomenon signify — A shift in political consciousness? A decline in the credibility of official channels of communication, including the mainstream mass media? The question deserves much more detailed study.

TRANSLATED BY SANDRA HAMID AND JOHN H. McGLYNN

AFRIZAL MALNA

Lumbering Oxen

Aboard a strange and foreign bus we leave darkened houses behind to embark on a journey towards new countries springing up along the road. Twilight is checked by the eerie glow of neon lights; all that remains of people are fleeting shadows. The journey becomes an ancient one, hurling us into the void of wordless creation. And when we accept the impossibility that the circular world is one endless and cyclical journey we jostle together as we depart from the end of one world to head towards the end of another. Who are we among the other peoples of the world.

Taken by the old and blustering arid wind, we are but dust that falls on dreams of mortality. Before the sun buries and drowns itself in the horizon we are but post scripts gaining a voice only after existence passes.

From Regions of Question

Where days are free from adornment, there we entertain new hopes that fleet across the television screens. And at this moment, too, our wives and children are dressed in clothes of yellow, red and blue. We switch to American dreams and see creatures who at every instant are transforming themselves. There, the city is an aquarium, inhabited by vicious alarm clocks. And we catch the fish that swim in industrial effluence. And then cheer for we can do anything with our bodies: be it carrying stones or stealing. But we cannot set prices. We don't know how we are suddenly suppose to change everything to money. And suddenly we have to search for ourselves in the middle of the market, the place where silence can change to anything, whenever. One day there came a dangerous place where not a single person could speak.

Asia Reads

Though the sun has changed so often here we still face the same sky and land. Asia. After the gods disappeared and were fossilized in television antennae, after times of destruction and old news harkened from another world, each word became pregnant with darkness. Thus we brought in new decor, of disharmony, to search for days in markets where dragon heads hang. Asia. Now we grope in games of power that lead to muteness. How are we to know that we are entering a world that reeks of gasoline, that we are setting free our children to play in reels of electric coil. In each page of the holy book we try once more to locate the moment of creation. The land which for ages has maintained us glistens with the smell of man. Asia. We understand once more the thunder of its sea, the place to which ancestors sent birds to create jungles. Asia can be found only in night's pitch darkness that roars in search of lost lands. Asia.

Myths of Regret

Our city is guarded by myths of regret. Weapons have transformed to memories inside our hearts that will once again create stories in moments of our longing. We have learned to read and to write but in frequent moments where comes the need to embrace days of absolute darkness we experience the blindness of illiteracy. We pray for the buffalo to make this earth tremble. For the birds to fly off in hunt through the sky. And then our mountains parade around the city. Our country becomes a jungle waiting for hotels to divide time. Oh, the dreams that now distribute themselves among unknown regions; who are the businessman that bought this land. We want to know where our children are dissolved in gasoline to keep the streets in constant agitation, thereby creating new cities the whole day long. And over the radio comes strange voices from rotting jungles, as if there is nothing else that tomorrow will bring.

My Girl

Oh, my girl, my girl, where have you gone. My girl has gone to lipstick city. My girl has gone to perfume city. My girl I'm sad your body is wrapped in neon. Your body eaten by stores. Don't leave your lips behind on the beach, my girl. The sea will later take you away; soap will take you away. My girl, that culture angrily devours you. My girl, your body carries a bed down the row of automobile lights, causing our mother to cry and to die. Don't fasten your breasts on the road signs, my girl. The police will be angry and you will die together with the radio. You will die buried beneath beauty parlors, my girl. You will die bitten by cats. All men become animals in the pitch darkness of night. Don't let your body be transformed to plastic, my girl. Your body, my god, your body is a ghost. None of us will later have a god. We will all be taken away by ghosts, my girl. We all love you. We all love you. Don't fly off with hotels, my girl. Don't take flight with restaurants, my girl. Our mother will die. Our mother will die. Our mother will die.

He Who Guards the Night

With the sea and mountains smelling of gasoline, the wind calls the birds to return home to the forest once more; the rain calls the fish to return home to the lakes. And the sleepless grass once more creates green fields, giving birth once more to a morning sun from a journey without end. It is there I retranslate myself into the crowd of people that reside in time, the place where earth gives birth to trees and mountains, where the sea gives birth to islands. There I meet he who forever guards the night, the place to which I return from every age, the place I marry my love. And people read themselves again as if opening the pages of books that must end. This is the place all prophets gather to receive everything, calling those names of ours hidden behind the dawn. And he who guards at night, his self is filled by prayer.

Morning Rain

Unlike we once imagined there is left but one reason in the world to explain our existence. Words pass by without even need of speakers. We stare and the mirror within ourselves is wet, like a puddle of water from old tales that no longer impart news. We hurriedly plant trees only to gaze at the distance between where we stand and the time that is spent destroying its bonds. All that is later made forms no reason to explain our days, that relate again the tales that we are not the center of everything. We smell the odor of our own bodies, and find it like the smell of medicine that once more nettles forth a story: no more is there flowing blood. No. We once made a house, a world, but then in surprise asked where we had to go home to. All that moves silently is changing itself, only to re-clarify the routes that we once passed.

Our Inheritance

Speak again my knife, my saw, my crowbar, my ax, my hammer, my chisel, my screwdriver, my pliers, my plane, my scissors, my rice sheath, my rice beater, my eaves trough.
Speak again my fields, my fish ponds, my rice barn, my granary, my goats, my bird cage, my buffalo pen, my kittens and cats, my cart, my bicycles, my flowers.
Speak again my house, my glass tiles, my windows, my fence, my dining table, my chairs, my bureau, my bed, my blanket, my coat, my sandals, my pens, my books.
Speak again my stove, my plates, my pans, my pots, my pails, my water pump, my drinking glasses, my tobacco, my pipe, my lighter. Speak again my mirror, my flashlight, my hat, my umbrella. Speak again my family, my ancestors, my friends and neighbors, as if telling your stories, that learn to read.

BONDAN WINARNO

Paris, April 29

AT THE DESERTED ALMA MARCEAU STATION Mahar stepped off the subway car of Metro Line No. 9 and was immediately slapped by the cold on the dimly lit platform. As he climbed the stairs he pulled his leather gloves out of his rain coat pocket.

On the main street in front of the Place de l'Alma the cold was even more biting. "A strange spring," Mahar thought. Gripping the edges of his rain jacket's lapels, he held his arms firmly across his chest. He crossed Avenue de New York, and moments later found himself on the Pont de l'Alma Bridge. The Seine flowed beneath him. At the center of the bridge he stopped to study the river's current then cocked his head towards the tip of the Eiffel Tower that soared across the way.

Paris, April 29 — a place and time that had come to form a kind of pilgrimage for Mahar in the last fifteen years. Time and again he had tried to break free from the guilt that ensnared him, but every time he tried, its hold seemed to grow stronger. Always Mahar was forced to accept his guilt and let himself be shackled again. This seemed to be the only way that he could make peace with his memories of Marie-Claire.

On April 29, 1975, Saigon fell to the Communists and in the mass evacuation that followed Mahar had been separated from Marie-Claire. "It will be only a little while, *ma cherrie*," he had told her when he left for the evacuation center at Tan Son Nhut Air Base. But Marie-Claire had just looked at him, blank eyed, as if she had nothing left to say.

Mahar tried to sound self assured: "We'll meet in Paris."

"I'm not going back to Paris," Marie-Claire countered. She pointed to the Saigon earth. "This is my home."

Mahar had never really understood Marie-Claire. She, like Bob Dylan and countless other members of her generation, was anti-establishment. She disliked even France and what she called its "Frenchness." She always wore the traditional *ao dai* and allowed the sun to darken her skin to conceal her fairness. She refused to live in the foreign enclave and, instead, rented a house near Alliance Française where she taught. The house was on Gia Long, a narrow and depressing lane lined with tamarind trees. She treated her maid, Mai Linh, like a close friend and emulated the bohemian life style of a true socialist.

"The war is going to get worse for you," Mahar whispered as he hugged Marie-Claire. "Sooner or later you are going to be chased out of Saigon."

Marie-Claire shook her head. "I'm a French citizen, Mahar, not American. I'm safe here."

Her stress on the words "not American" annoyed Mahar. There was a note of sharpness he did not like.

Mahar kissed Marie-Claire then jumped into the waiting jeep. A tamarind fruit fell and cracked open on the helmet he had just put on. Marie-Claire, with Mai Linh behind her, stood straight and stiff, showing no change of emotion. No tears were on her cheeks.

Mahar was despondent. He suddenly had a lump in his throat. "Until we meet again, *ma cherrie. . .*"

"When you return to Saigon. . ." Marie-Claire answered resolutely. She then raised her arm and waved in the direction of the jeep that took Mahar away.

That was Mahar's last vision of Marie-Claire: standing in a white *ao dai*, beneath a tamarind tree, rigid and without tears.

IT WAS AT TAN SON NHUT that Mahar realized the truth of Marie-Claire's words: only Americans were in danger. Fifteen thousand French citizens with not more than a dozen gendarmes to protect them stood fast in Vietnam. The United States was the Viet Cong's enemy, not the people of other nations.

"Don't think of yourself as American," Pierre Brochand, Assistant to the French Ambassador in Saigon told him when they met outside the Hotel Caravelle.

"But the Viet Cong know that I work for an American magazine," Mahar protested.

"Your skin is brown," Pierre stressed. "And don't forget, though I can't absolutely guarantee your safety, I can help you."

Pierre's offer shook Mahar's assurance. Maybe he should stay in Saigon.

"You're crazy!" an American intelligence officer told him. "The Communists are already camped in the jungle north of Saigon, between Ben Cat and the Michelin Rubber Plantation. We're not counting days before Saigon falls but minutes and seconds."

Mahar was even more confused.

"The Communists are color-blind, Mahar," added a black American pilot. "They don't care what color you are. '*Time*, Capitalist Magazine' is written on your forehead. Get real, Mahar, and get out of here!"

So Mahar boarded the truck that took him back to Saigon and to the United States embassy complex. Hundreds of Vietnamese who had been promised passage out of the country were climbing the high walls to get inside. Mahar was pushed into a Chinook CH-53 helicopter, the last to leave Saigon. It flew straight to the open sea.

Once on board the USS Okinawa Mahar learned that not all the foreign correspondents had left Saigon. Peter Arnett was still there, as was Don Harris from NBC. Mahar's panic to save himself had dulled his better judgment.

"Coward," Mahar ridiculed himself. He thought of Marie-Claire standing beneath the tamarind tree. "Now that's courage."

MAHAR WALKED ACROSS QUAY D'ORSAY, and entered Avenue Bosquet. Spring was apparent in the green of the trees along the street. He turned onto Cognacq Jay, crossed the grounds of Television Française on "TF-1" and came to the end of the street where it intersected Jean-Nicot. He turned right and stopped in front of house number twenty-three.

On the maroon door frame was a symbol engraved in gilt: a pen tip wrapped in barbed wire. He knocked.

The door was thrown open. Yves Dutertre instantly threw his arms around Mahar and pulled him inside where he shook hands with several people he did not know and hugged the ones he did, all of them journalists who had been stationed in Saigon in the early 1970s. On April 29 of each year they gathered in Paris to mark the fall of Saigon, an occasion never commemorated in the United States.

"American journalists aren't romantic at all," Yves had to say. "The only thing they care about is higher salaries."

Mahar laughed but wondered if Yves had forgotten or did not realize that he himself still worked as a reporter in the States.

"It's not that," Mahar said to Yves. "Memories of the day are far too bitter for most Americans."

Yves steered Mahar to a bar in the corner where he began to make a gin and tonic.

"Did you cover the Gulf War?"

Mahar shook his head. "I'm too old to be on the front line."

"But Peter Arnett got himself quite a name there, didn't he?" Yves asked as he handed Mahar the gin and tonic.

"And a new wife as well," Mahar added.

BOTH THE TWO MEN had known Arnett in Saigon. Yves had been a cameraman for TF-1 and was just one of the many foreign correspondents who had fallen in love with Peter's sister-in-law, a stunning Vietnamese beauty. Arnett had made the most of his situation to call attention to himself and on social occasions had not only brought his pretty wife but his sister-in-law, too. Flanked by two lovely women, he seemed to savor the jealous looks of his many jealous colleagues.

It was Yves who had first put Mahar into contact with Marie-Claire. At that time she was the girlfriend of Tiziano Terzani, an Italian communist reporter. Mahar was head over heals for Marie-Claire and could not understand how she could fall for such a bear as Tiziano. Later, when Tiziano was run out of Saigon, people said it was because of pressure from the U.S. Press Attaché.

"If you want to get close to Marie-Claire," Yves advised, "whatever you do, don't act like a capitalist!"

Mahar tried conjuring ways of getting to know Marie-Claire. He eventually found a solution: he asked her to serve as an interpreter in an interview with a South Vietnamese officer who spoke only French. In that interview Mahar had succeeded in getting the officer to admitting that American medical supplies were being sold to the black market which had become a strategic supply line for the North Vietnamese military.

"It won't be easy to get this report accepted," Mahar told Marie-Claire after the officer left. "These kinds of things infuriate the brass in the Pentagon."

Marie-Claire looked at Mahar sympathetically. "So, the American press also thinks of the Pentagon's interests?"

"Well, this is war," Mahar commented, feeling his hook catch.

That night they ate dinner at Ny Khanh, a floating restaurant on the river at the end of Nguyen Hue Boulevard. The candle light made Marie-Claire's brown eyes look like the eyes of a Bengalese tiger. They seemed to dance when Mahar talked about the racism he experienced in America.

"Yes, racism is alive and well in the United States," Mahar stated.

"And equality is but an empty phrase in France," Marie-Claire added.

Marie-Claire became further attracted to Mahar when he told her about the books of John Dos Pasos, the Harvard graduate who in World War I had served as ambulance driver in Europe. His novels about America showed the writer to hold very socialist views. By the time they were walking along the river bank in front of Hotel Majestic the two were already holding hands.

Yve's advice to Mahar turned out to be very useful. Mahar went on to talk about the changing attitudes of American journalists who were stationed in Saigon. President Carter had given the American mass media the opportunity to be more honest in their coverage of the war. As a result, an open debate was going on in the United States about its military interests in Vietnam. This development was not at all appealing to the Pentagon.

On Tu Do Street Marie-Claire put her arm around Mahar's waist. Mahar returned the favor and put his arm around her too. He felt, beneath her thin cotton *ao dai*, a slight shiver run through her body.

Mahar then told her about Indonesia: about a village at the foot of Mount Salak, about fancy houses being built on the mountain sides, about farmers who sold their land to become laborers in the city — about the transformation from one kind of poverty to another.

Beneath an acacia tree in front of Our Lady of Peace Basilica, Mahar kissed Marie-Claire's cheek and then her lips. "I love you," he whispered.

Marie-Claire stared at him sadly. "Don't say that, Mahar. We're just two lonely creatures thrown together by circumstance. Situations always change. . ."

"How very honest of you, Marie Claire," Mahar said to himself.

WHEN ANOTHER GUEST KNOCKED, Yves left Mahar standing in the corner of the room. Mahar took his glass and joined a Canadian journalist who had just returned from covering the Gulf War. The man had been a junior reporter when Mahar knew him in Saigon. Mahar had seen him several times at the Associated Press office at the Hotel Caravelle. The office of *Time*, where he worked, was at the Continental Palace Hotel which was located almost next door to Hotel Caravelle, separated only by the National Assembly building. The AP office was a rendezvous point for foreign corespondents. Another popular meeting place was the Jerome and Juliette Bar found in the same hotel.

"You can't judge someone's ability by his age," Marie-Claire once said to Mahar in that bar. They were talking about the Canadian reporter.

Mahar had just returned from Da Nag at that time. The North Vietnamese had bombed Da Nag Harbor to ruins. In the attack, the North Vietnamese had even used A37s and C130s, stolen property from the U.S. Air Force. The bombing had resulted in a large-scale evacuation of American personnel from Da Nag. It had been a field day for correspondents. During the bombing, the Canadian writer had hidden in a bomb shelter, and there had been hit by a Viet Cong sniper bullet. Luckily it had only grazed his cheek.

MARIE-CLAIRE ALWAYS STOOD on the side of the defenseless. Her servant, Mai Linh, was one example. Mai Linh had been a washwoman at the American service personnel apartments on Tu Do Street, not far from the Alliançe Française. Naive Mai Linh had not understand that she had rights, too, and that as a washwoman it was not her duty to fill the sexual needs of the American personnel. All she knew was that in doing so she was able to bring home more money and sometimes even American cigarettes for her father.

It was Marie-Claire who had "saved" Mai Linh and who had given Mai Linh a room in her apartment, one the same size as her own, with furniture of the same quality. Mai Linh ate at the same table as Marie-Claire, even when Mahar was visiting. At night, Marie-Claire taught Mai Linh both French and mathematics.

"I'm not a communist," Marie-Claire had said to Mahar on a separate occasion, "but I'm not a colonialist or a capitalist either. I hate seeing people exploited by others, especially by foreigners who think that their white skin gives them permission to stand above the suffering of a less fortunate race."

Her brown eyes glistened, their beam drilled into Mahar's eyes. Mahar clasped Marie-Claire's hand. They passed the Mariners' Statue outside Hotel Catinant. Tu Do Street was deserted when they crossed it and entered the Continental Palace Hotel lobby.

The fans spinning on the ceiling of Mahar's room could not cool the hot April night. Marie-Claire took off her *ao dai*. Her sudden nakedness caught Mahar by surprise.

"Take off your clothes," she told him. "This heat. . ."

And they made love beneath the lazily spinning fans.

"I love you Marie-Claire," Mahar told Marie-Claire again as he held her hand.

Marie-Claire stared at him with beauty in her eyes. "Don't say that unless you truly mean it. Let's just do it; we both need it."

"I really do love you," Mahar repeated. And though she never told him that she loved him, Mahar concluded on his own that she did.

AND PERHAPS, IN HER OWN WAY, Marie-Claire did love him. "I'm afraid of losing you," she had told him after his return from Camp Davis, moniker for the barracks at Tan So Nhut Harbor where the North Vietnamese and South Vietnamese were trying to negotiate a peace accord.

Marie-Claire wiped the sweat from Mahar's forehead with the hem of her *ao dai*. Mahar's motorcycle was suddenly toppled by a large dog running through the lane but Mahar let it lie. Other things were on his mind. Nguyen Van Thieu had resigned and Tran Van Huong replaced him as President of South Vietnam.

"How is Old Man Tran going to save South Vietnam," Marie-Claire said, more as a statement than a question.

Mahar shook his head as he gulped down the ice tea that Mai Linh brought down to him.

It was now a public secret: Saigon was on the threshold of destruction. Communist forces were massed at New Port Bridge while at Camp Davis, Mahar had learned, North Vietnam was refusing to negotiate with Trans Van Huong.

After Mai Linh had gone to the back of the house Marie-Claire sat down on Mahar's lap. This was the first time Marie-Claire had shown sentimentality. She looked at Mahar's tired face then dropped her head onto his shoulder.

"You're not afraid of losing me, are you?"

Her question was almost a whisper.

Mahar caressed Marie-Claire's back. "We all have reason to be afraid, *ma cherrie*."

MAHAR TURNED DOWN YVES' OFFER to walk him home. He wanted the loneliness to himself, and for his memories of Marie-Claire.

Mahar slowly crossed Pont de l'Alma Bridge, no longer aware of the cold night air. In the middle of the bridge he stopped to study once more the Seine's languid flow.

"No, you'll never die, Marie-Claire," Mahar whispered. "You'll always live inside me."

TRANSLATED BY LISA C. HO

BONDAN WINARNO

Abus

IF FATHER HADN'T FORCED ME, I would never have studied the Koran under Abus. Never. Abus wasn't my teacher's real name. Everyone honored him with the Arabic title "Abu," but Father told me his real name was Bustomi. He himself called him Abu. Even my grandfather called him Abu. So, we children never called him anything else, either. People called him Abu Bus, from Abu Bustomi, to distinguish him from others with the title Abu. And that's how the venerable Mr Bustomi ended up with the name Abus.

When I was only nine years old, Abus was already eighty-one. Nine times older than I was. Imagine! It wasn't surprising that he always treated me disparagingly. In his presence, I was always a bumbler. I could never hold my pen the right way when writing the Arabic alphabet. And I was even worse when I had to read from the Koran. Whatever I did, something would be wrong.

I didn't like Abus. Neither did any of my friends of my age. But no matter how hard we worked together, we could never do anything to him. Our parents would always side with Abus against us. In my own home town of Petakan, Abus was always right. If there was ever any trouble at the prayer-house, it had to be the fault of the children. No one would ever have blamed Abus. In short, Abus was the Ayatollah of Petakan.

Abus was thought to be the oldest person of sound mind in the village. To be sure, Mak Nung was older than he was but she passed her days without rising from her bed, which made her quite different from Abus.

Abus lived two lives. The first was in the prayer-house where he led the prayers and taught the Koran. Even though he had never in his life been married, people said that there was no better counselor around for giving advice to married couples who were going through difficult times. And maybe because of Abus' services, there were never any divorces in Petakan, only marriages.

His other life was as a *bubur* vendor, selling black-rice pudding. At three in the morning he was already up, preparing the coconut milk, dissolving the palm-sugar, and boiling up the sticky black rice, the green beans, and regular white rice in big pots. Then, after leading the morning prayer, he would set up his humble business on a low table in front of the prayer-house.

Maybe Abus had happened to read a book on sales techniques. When he was selling *bubur*, he always had a smile for everyone. His *bubur*, which was actually very good, sold well; his smile always enticed customers to purchase a second helping. In the prayer-house, however, the smile would disappear from his face. Every day, except during the fasting month of Ramadan, Abus wore these two different faces.

I remember one time Abus belted me with his rattan stick. Whack! Right across my spine, on the thirteenth vertebrae. I didn't cry, no way, I was ten years old at that time. But my pride was certainly hurt. I had thought that by my age, I wouldn't be treated like a little child any more. And yet, Abus had beaten me. Even my own father didn't hit me anymore.

After that incident I thought for a long time about how to pay Abus back for my humiliation. Finally, I came up with an idea: Abus was obsessed with his *siawak*. Do you know what a *siawak* is? You might be revolted if I tell you, but if I don't you won't understand how I planned to take my revenge. Anyway, a *siawak* is an Arabian tooth-brush, made from a short stick of wood with one of the ends crushed to form a kind of brush. Once, when Abus went on the pilgrimage, he saw that the Arabs always cleaned their teeth with such a brush before they performed their prayers. So he came to the conclusion that his prayers would be legitimate only if he first brushed his teeth with a *siawak*, too. You can imagine how bad it smelt after it had been used over and over again.

Abus never threw his brushes away. He had made the pilgrimage six times, and each time he had returned with a new brush. Everyone in the village who went on the pilgrimage knew that the way to make Abus happy was to bring him back a new *siawak*. He kept all his brushes in one of the staves of bamboo that formed part of the wall of the prayer-house, near the spot where he led the daily prayers.

One night, after the evening prayer, I stole one of his brushes and took it back home with me. The next day, before leaving for morning prayer, I poured out a mound of chili powder and pepper, and rubbed the brush into the deadly pile. I was the first one to arrive at the prayer house and I put the spiked brush back in the place where Abus was most likely to reach for it.

By the time Abus came, another ten or so children were there, ready for the morning prayer. I tensed when I saw Abus choosing a brush but breathed with relief when he chose the one I had fixed for him. Unsuspecting, he began to clean his teeth. A moment later he frowned. His eyes bulged. And then he hurled the brush down onto the prayer-mat. As his mouth burned, his curses grew louder and louder.

I ran out helter-skelter with the other kids. There was no way that Abus, who was eighty-two at the time, could hope to catch us. We kids were out of control that morning. Everyone was frantically trying to guess who had doctored the brush but no one was admitting to it. I certainly wasn't going to. And there was nothing to be gained by casting suspicion on anyone else because most all of us had reason to bear a grudge against Abus.

Because of what had happened none of us had the courage to buy Abus' delicious *bubur*, and I went on to school with a very hungry stomach. I kept myself going by putting some fried taro into my stomach at break time.

None of the kids went back to the prayer-house that day. Not for the afternoon prayer, not for the twilight prayer, and not for the evening prayer either.

When my father heard what had happened he asked me if it was I who had done such a wicked thing. Lucky for me my father was easily convinced that I hadn't. Father always preferred to be proud of me.

As it happened, a week passed, and still not a single child had found the courage to return to the prayer-house. My father tried coaxing me into going back, but I didn't want to at all.

"If I go by myself and the other kids aren't there, Abus will probably thrash the daylights out of me!"

My father tried to sway my opinion: "At most he'll be angry for a while. You can put up with that. As an older man who deserves respect, he feels that you kids have played an unpleasant prank on him. You'll just have to get over it and face the consequences like a man!"

"But when Abus beats you he goes completely out of control," I protested. "If he tries to take a stick to my butt, he's just as likely to hit me in the eyes and blind me!"

Maybe the idea of me, his one and only male child, beeing blinded, gave my father cause for anxiety, for after that, he offered his services as a peace-maker. He urged all the children of Petakan to come and face Abus together in the prayer-house. And Abus couldn't be angry, because my father gave a very fine speech of apology on behalf of all the children. Abus accepted our apologies. Then, we, one by one, filed by to kiss his hand.

How were we to know that Abus' desire for revenge was greater than his sense of forgiveness? The next morning we gathered together, waiting for Abus to lead the morning prayer. All of us were there. It was only Abus who hadn't come. Suddenly, we heard the door of the prayer-house being shut from outside. And then, *click*!, it was locked as well. Abus had locked us into the prayer-house. And he just left us there. That was his revenge.

Maybe I'm not the heroic type because I never did own up to doing what I had done with that *siawak*. When it came around to Idul Fitri and you're suppose to ask forgiveness for your wrong doings, I gave a lot of thought to owning up but, in the end, I didn't have the courage to say anything. I kept my secret to myself.

I already said that Abus had made the pilgrimage six times. That's right. Not that he was the richest man in the village. I mean, have you ever known a rich *bubur* vendor? But Abus was the most frugal man in the village and he saved all his money. His *sarong* was stitched and patched and he never ate meat, except maybe on Idul Fitri and Kenduri when it was given to him. He hid all the money he earned from selling *bubur* and the fees that were paid to him by his students in the bamboo joints of his house. And when the time came, he would split the bamboo open, and count his savings. He'd use this money to finance his pilgrimage and pay the Pilgrimage Fee.

And that's what he did when he turned eighty-three. I, of all people, helped him split the bamboo open and count his money. I was the best student of arithmetic in Petakan. And Abus knew that. I counted his money. He had more than enough for the pilgrimage fee.

"Praise be to Allah!" he shrieked, throwing his hands in the air. And then he began to cry.

The night before he left for the Holy Land, Abus suddenly asked that the *tahlil*, the last rites, be read for him. His request unnerved us.

"Just think of me as dead," he told us, "but read the *tahlil* for me."

Abus had always said that he wanted to die in the Holy Land. Everyone had heard him say it. And now he was eighty-three years old, and going on the pilgrimage for the seventh time.

"I may never return," he said.

The next morning the whole village turned out to see him off at Poncol Station. And there we were, all of us taking leave of a man going off to die. Abus didn't cry, but there were many among us who did. When he was leaving, I almost ran to him to kiss his hand and tell him that it had been I who had spiked his brush with pepper and chili. Before he died, I thought, he should know my secret.

But then you have to remember: I was only eleven years old, and in the end I didn't tell him anything and kept the secret to myself.

And Abus didn't come back. We all thought he had passed away in the Holy Land, just as he had wished. I began to regret that I had not asked him for his forgiveness and often, when I performed my prayers, I prayed that Abus was at peace by God's side and had forgotten my trespass against him.

Each year thereafter, whenever people from the village made the pilgrimage they were always told to find out what had happened to Abus. That if he had died, they were to pay their respects at his grave. But no one ever came back from the trip with news of him.

One day, when I was eighteen, which was about seven years after Abus' departure, an old man suddenly showed up at our village. He wore a black cloak and was very decrepit but looked a lot like Abus. Who was he? Everyone wanted to know. Was it Abus or, maybe, Abus' ghost?

The onlookers stood stiff and silent as the black-robed figure hobbled along the lane towards Abus' old house which was now being used by our new religious teacher.

My father was the first to have the courage to greet the ghost. "*Assalamualaikum*. Peace be with you!" my father said in greeting. "Are you Abu Bustomi?"

Everyone looked on nervously from a distance. The figure nodded its head slowly and my father kissed his hand. Abus pulled my father towards him and embraced him.

"Abus has returned! Abus has returned!" my father shouted.

Now everyone approached, pushing one another forward to greet Abus and kiss his hand. Poor Abus, so old and feeble — Don't forget, he was ninety years old — was obviously touched.

He hadn't died. That meant I still had time to ask his forgiveness for the incident with the tooth-brush. Now, at eighteen, I had the courage to do it, even if it meant a beating.

Father invited Abus to stay at our house, and when Mother asked him what had made him come back to his birth-place, his eyes filled with tears.

"Your *sayur lodeh* and salted fish," he told my mother haltingly.

So Mother immediately set to preparing vegetables for *sayur lodeh* and frying up some salted fish. Our new religious teacher and several of the other elders were invited to lunch together with Abus. I wasn't going to be allowed to sit and eat with them, that was certain, but I stuck around to help Mother, scurrying back and forth between the kitchen and the dining room.

Abus ate ravenously. His appetite was truly phenomenal. His forehead broke out in a sweat. Father put more rice and *sayur lodeh* on his plate and offered him more salted fish, which he accepted happily. The more he ate the more his forehead sweat. Everyone was happy to see him. He wasn't dead at all. On the contrary, he was here, beside us, with an astounding appetite.

When he finally finished eating Abus appeared quite breathless.

"Thank you, Icah. That was an outstanding meal," he praised my mother. "For seven years I've been longing for food like that."

Mother just nodded in response but I could see tears at the corners of her eyes.

Abus leaned against the wall while he fanned his face with a newspaper. He belched, then cried out "Praise be to God." For a moment he was silent but then cried out again: "God is great!" He then collapsed at my father's side. Father jumped forward, but Abus was already gone. Only his corpse remained, lifeless in my father's arms. Once again, I had missed the opportunity to ask him for his forgiveness. I stood in a daze as the rest of the people rushed around making arrangements for Abus' funeral. And finally, when his corpse was left alone for a moment on the mat still littered with dirty dishes, I knelt down and kissed his hands which had been entwined on top of his chest. I whispered into his ear, begging him to forgive me. I thought that maybe, just maybe he might still hear me. After all, his spirit could surely have not gone very far.

TRANSLATED BY TIM KORTSCHAK

DANARTO

Adam Enlightened

I AM THE LIGHT THAT, rolling along at 300,000 kilometers per hour, reveals the morning, and it is called morning, that raises the sun overhead, and it is called midday, that throws it westwards and you call it afternoon, the smouldering orb sinks beneath the ocean, the damascened waves sparkle with silver, while the shore runs like a brushstroke towards infinity, grey and irregular, yet you ask where I reside; I AM light, skimming along at 300,000 kilometers per second, even in those dark regions that you name night I am wont to float, drifting between midnight and dawn, resist the habit of going early to bed and you will see me burst open, a seed to send forth its first sprout, see me cause its tender stalk to snake upwards, send out creepers, lengthen until its tip dangles downwards like some soft and verdant ornament, I am also he who causes turtles' eggs to hatch at the beach — see the hatchlings there, still swathed in mucous as the sea foam laps and laps about them? in the same way I shepherded the elements on their journey to monocellular life, and I make the down that covers your body grow, each instant each strand lengthens a bit, and of course each one gibbers on to me — I talk endlessly to them, and likewise to your hands, feet, eyes, nose, ears, mouth, privates, and anus, all of which tend to have more things to talk about than you do yourself, hearing this you wonder who or what your integral self is: you are the sum of your discoveries while I am my secret undiscovery: I AM light streaking at the speed of thought, dazzling, polychrome, a rainbow curving from continent to continent, nothing within your comprehension can match my speed, yet at the same time I am the architect of your brain, and I have connected it to the central office where I manage things, oh so gingerly, the floating clouds, the rain I cause to fall, the stars I have placed just so to avoid their constantly bumping into each other, all of these are lovely celestial decorations, but at the same time one of that vast array of sources of scientific knowledge which from year to year drives your intellectual advancement forward as before a steadily blowing wind, but wait, when I first formed you, I wrapped you in my light, so warm, a bundle of love — you've sat watching a drizzling rain through a window, haven't you? that's the feeling I'm talking about, a mixture of the homey warmth of the room and the cold air streaming over the window sill, of the desire to dash out and play as you remember doing in your youth and the desire to dwell in the warm room of adulthood, take these all and mix them well until you can't tell one from the other, that really is my best analogy, you understand now, but me, I must continue my journey, for my labor continues through all the ages, nor am I ever fatigued, for I AM light, forever flying, and even in my stillness I continue to fly, whatever I pass on my journey, I greet it, and repair it if something is amiss, this is a statement of fundamental truth, mark it, for whatever else you are, you are my creature, and at one point you were like wind in my hand: meaningless, but wait, what is it I said before: I AM a constantly flowing wind moving at unimaginable speed, I am harsh, so that you have the saying "a forceful wind", truly that is me: I endlessly exchange stale air for fresh, I am a balmy breeze, I am a whirlwind, I am a storm, I am a hurricane, and all of these I swallow with the same ease that you draw breath, I enter your lungs through your nose, I pump your heart, then riding on your blood I play with your glands until you are hot and excited, or I stroke your face until it reddens and your breath is whistling, I massage your sinews, I blow into your marrow till your bones expand, enlarge, assume their proper proportions of beauty and loveliness, I work your digits, fingers and toes, like a masseur, ah yes, caressing your hair, whispering into your ear, the fact is you are only alive because you consume air, your lungs are a factory operating all day and I work for you there, you don't want to break for even a minute to have a look outside, such is your dedication, but I stream out through your pores and when I fill my chest it makes your gait unsteady so that often you take off, fly up, leaving the ground behind, often you perform beyond the limits of your abilities, often you eat more than your stomach can hold, often you sleep more deeply than you should be able, I am the one who arranges all such occurrences, one day a very unexpected thing will happen, it won't be a freak accident, but something that arises naturally, a formula that I will push you to record because it can be expressed as a formula, for I AM the wind, I breathe over the universe and it expands, stars orbit stars, I reside at the center of all this, blowing, blowing, and the cosmos likewise breathes, in and out, in and out, in and out, you are my microcosm, whom I love, and with your breathing your village, your city, also draws air and expels, draws air and expels, draws air and expels, this labor is easy for me, easy for you, even in moments of carelessness you continue naturally to respirate: I blow into the fetus in the womb, from instant to instant, it develops, I sit by its side, I rock it, sometimes it rolls around like an inanimate object, sometimes it is like an old person, but I AM fire: my breath is the noble prophet Jesus, Jacob is my hearing, Joseph my visage, David my voice, Solomon my power, Abraham my soul, Enoch my hair, Sayyid Ali my skin, Abu Bakar my blood, my flesh Omar, my bones his majesty Othman, my marrow Fatimah the noble, Aminah my vitality, Job my entrails, and all the hair that grew on the Prophet's body grows also on mine, my light is Muhammad, my insight the Emissary, suffice it to say that all the prophets and saints are united within my spiritual-corporal being, I am the life force, I am the oversoul, I am creativity, I am the Creator, I am passion, I am effort, I am counterpoised exertions, I am steadiness, I am the power of thought and action, I am the spirit of religion, art, and love, I am lust, I am anger, the convincing power of destruction, I am wars, I am famine, I am ignorance, I am intelligence, I am the power of growth and annihilation, I am the spirit of nature that distills knowledge into your brain, I am process, gaze into the mirror of my being and you will see nothing there but me, my face reflected in every detail like yours, indeed all of creation is simply a probationary test, all of it will in the end reunite with me, all of it is my blood, I flow in your blood, I smoulder in your blood, I once dreamt about red blood — so I created red blood, whereas I had once dreamt of white blood — so I created white blood, now when these two types greet each other, on male, the other female, and I arise from the conjunction,

"who are you?"

"I am red blood,"

"who are you?"

"I am white blood,"

but I in fact am blue blood, brown blood, black blood, vermilion, violet, gray, yellow, I am rainbow blood, life's glowing ember, my sleep is wakefulness, my waking is sleep, I sail in the blood, my ark is blood, my sea is blood, my wind is blood, my breath is blood, a spark of flame shoots up as from a flint and over there the place you are flocking is lit up, I light a fire for your bed clothes — illumination — and the center remains, I am your pole star, your point of orientation, the destination of your travels, for I AM the flame, you the nocturnal termite inexorably drawn, yet we are identical, you are the visible me, I the invisible you, all of you shall become me, so that in reality there is no trial or test, that's all silliness, yes, I am silliness, I am tomfoolery, I am cluelessness, I am naiveté I am hilarity, I am emptiness, the void of meaning, absolute stillness, you are often cast upon me who makes you sad, despairing, angry, and then I flood your blood with my flames, but really I AM water, the source of your existence, once I blew into the belly of a mountain which you then drilled into and discovered a priceless treasure, overflowing, you who originated from a dot that was expelled in a gush — after which you gestated and grew until, overflowing, you thundered out and flooded the plains, then new seeds grew in the still moist mud, beneath searing heat, and I evaporated then rolled over and over, then descended again, all of which reminds you of your childhood, how you enjoyed that game, while I made waves, rippled, the pool seeming so vast, its depth unfathomable, an element hard yet soft, I babbled along, you ran on tippy-toes, having fun at your play, a sea is a sea, a river a river, and a seed, yes, a seed, and you wonder — all you do is wonder — what was water before it was water? you explain it in your own way, when in the morning you find vestiges of dew or haze still hovering you quickly trap it, take it inside, and for a full day, and the next day too, you are immersed in the dew, diving deep into it with a grapple in your hand, of course there are some objects there that you manage to hook, you appear to drown, a mirror presents itself: you see nothing but me in your reflection, so that all at once you are consumed in flame, air bubbles shoot upwards, bursting from the water's surface, you are the ghostly floaters that hover mirage-like within the eyeball, visible yet invisible, as the rest of you jostle to make your way in to replace him, immersed in a drop of dew upon an early dawn, and thus you erupt in flames again and unite with the air, at one with each other, but this is a noble tradition, so others still in their thousands come on in your stead, then I shout: "you are water," they are transfixed in front without making it all the way, they all catch fire and burn until they melt and run and become one with the dew that they had sought to investigate, and that dew remains, as ever, my secret, others come in their millions, and I leave them undisturbed with their multitudes of conclusions, I like it that way, why not, from time to time they argue, that's fine, and I am left to myself untouched, unchanged, then suddenly they leap up even higher, but I am higher still, from age to age I flow without ceasing, always changing, always new, I am newness, you sample me and I taste different today than yesterday, but I AM earth; first, a pre-made armature, built of rebar intertwined with wire, straightened, bent, lengthened, clipped short, founded in beauty and harmony, which later you fill with me, fistful by fistful, often casting me from a moderate distance, making me leap, grab the wire, bite it, smother it, while your skilled hands mold and form, and the I that is you comes into being, a handsome creation, from earth, from earth, from earth,

earth, I am the one who understands the situation, piled on top of a bus in a jumble of other cargo, until I reach a large terminal, perhaps the largest, and the bus I'm riding on pulls up and stops among the rows of other buses, while on the other side of the station numerous municipal buses come and go, all of them vastly overloaded, to the point that they're bottoming out and riding all tilted, and after they spew out their passengers they ride upright again, until they become bloated from swallowing more passengers, and move out heavy and tilting again, I smile for a moment on the roof of my bus while the baggage battened down around me is untied and unloaded, I feel shaky for a minute since I'm really part of the baggage — but not really baggage, often I load stuff up or hand it down, I mention my destination, only I don't shout it out, but it's clear and understandable even in the midst of the events of the moment, though in fact I do it very quietly, this is a bus terminal where the rules hold, and all the passengers realize it, they queue up, they advance, they retreat, a few struggle to break free, but that isn't allowed, everything has been thought through and planned ahead of time, that's the way it has to be if you want things to run smoothly, people aren't allowed to jump from one bus to another, except for me as I am usually invisible to them, from being a pile of sacks I change shape and become a light plastic package the kids selling newspapers fight over, scrambling to take possession, then I transform into a kite carried aloft by the wind, swift and high, which the kids now chase with no regard for the traffic, until I'm snagged by a big tamarind tree and am stuck, here, in front of the best hotel, and the kids faces fall and they go away disappointed, so I dematerialize then rematerialize again on a bus, I understand the situation, for me it's like reading the newspaper, everything is spread out nice and plain in front of me, I see that more and more buses are needed to handle increasing numbers of passengers, the buses are always loaded down, always full, always overflowing with passengers, I smile seeing all of this, I want to make many buses to accommodate all of you while keeping the fares low, I want to be the gardener who cares for the terminal grounds, to make everything grow tall and shady, sending out green cool leaves to counteract the smell of diesel fumes and the hot air, I want to make bus travel easier still, see, I heed even the smallest things, so I jump upon a tall monument, gain an even clearer view, with one event following another and another, but my conclusion is unchanged: you still need more buses, and I, Adam Enlightened, who understands the situation, who trembles upon a monument, over a fountain, in houses of finance, in presidential palaces, in heroes' graves, in slums, in mansions, in field and factory, now I stand up upon a bus and shout, ". " and those who are about to leave and those who have just arrived on the buses, stop for a moment, before one or two approach the bus I'm standing on, so I shout once again: ". " and then a crowd begins to form, growing larger by the minute, surrounding me, until finally it overruns my bus,

"who are you!" they demand

"Adam Enlightened" I respond

"what are you up to"

"I am about to utter the divine word" I respond

"are you a prophet?" they demand

"no"

"are you a divinity?"

"no"

"what then?"

"I am neither prophet nor divinity, I am only Allah come to earth" I respond

"what the hell. . . ."

they are incensed, and each of them, in their countless numbers, takes up a stone,

"but I am a mango tree" I shout, they throw their stones against the mango tree that, heavy with fruit, stands atop a bus, all the fruit fall from the tree, but the number of mangos has been calculated so that their total is equivalent to the number of stones that were thrown, so no one needs to fight over the fruit, and all is well because the mangos fall precisely into each person's hand, and now everyone is enjoying the delicious fruit, and then falls asleep, changing the terminal into an expansive bed, the melting tar solidifies, some of them snore and the buses being held up by the sleepers also snore, further blocking the way, forcing new buses that pull up to stop outside, and stand in line, their drivers and conductors furious, their passengers furious, and crowding their way in intending to upbraid the people who have lain down and gone to sleep with no regard for anyone else, but as soon as they see the mango tree on the bus they are intrigued, they approach it, hop-skotching over the sleepers, when all at once the mango bursts into fruit,

"hey!" they shout, gathering up rocks,

and they pelt the tree, but once again the tree has calculated the number of people throwing stones so it can repay with the same number of mangos, they each receive a mango right in their hand, which they eat, become drowsy and fall asleep, time passes and more and more buses are lined up outside, more and more people are scattered about looking at the mango tree, among them armed police officers who enter, cock their rifles, fire their rifles all together into the air, but even with that the sleepers aren't disturbed, not the tiniest bit, so the effort to rouse them has failed, then seeing the mango tree atop the bus they cock their rifles again, but almost immediately lower them at the order of their commander, it seems it's bad form to shoot a tree, they approach the tree and suddenly it is laden with fruit again, more than before, but the police don't seem to know what to do with the luscious fruit, so they just stand there, this makes the tree smile, the shrill sound of sirens approaches, fire trucks come speeding up with teams of fire fighters hanging haphazardly on their sides, they jump down and skilfully unroll and hook up the hoses, now the water shoots out, pounding the sleepers, but they are truly in the grip of their dreams, or something, and the spray of the hoses, heavy as a thunderstorm, doesn't faze them, till the water runs out leaving the firefighters puzzled, the chief steps forward, orders his men to move people out of the way, they pile them up so that their snoring takes on the sound of a choir, and now the fire trucks can pass, they surround the mango tree, at the touch of a button the hook-and-ladder swings into action, squeaking upwards towards the tree trunk and the brave firefighters pick its fruit while below the police are shouting divvy it up guys, at this point the tree presents fruit tailored to the numbers of policemen, and the whole thing ends with everyone falling asleep, creating a moment of perfect calm, undoubtedly the first time a bus terminal in a big city turned into a baby's crib and ushered in tranquillity, even the air is clean, I rise slowly and change the tree back into myself, I slowly take the asphalt surface of the terminal, fold up its ends, curve the sides up, the storied building in the center I split up, balancing its parts evenly around the sides, the front and back, till I've made a boat of moderately large proportions, I command the winds to blow strongly to drive the boat, since all the seamen are still fast asleep, a shiver is felt, we begin slowly to move, suddenly one or two people are roused, startled, surprised, rather frightened, with the result that they jump off the boat and go running off towards the main road, but the boat sails along, moving down the streets with no trouble, eventually building to a fast clip, a few more people jump off this way and that, of course I let them, no need to entice them to stay with sweetly overripe mangos, they're free, everyone is free and I freed them, to tell you the truth I even shout at the ones I see just sitting lazily back,

"if you don't like this trip you're free to get off,"

but they just smile at me, the boat speeds on, it goes without saying that with this many passengers I have to provide everything, so they can shower with water fit for showering, eat food suitable for eating, dress themselves with clothing suitable for wear, sleep in appropriate accommodations, as the day wears into afternoon everyone takes a refreshing shower just like at home and I serve dinner at a long table covered with an unornamented white tablecloth, the fare properly nutritious of course,

"please enjoy the meal" I say, gesturing for them to begin, which they do with relish, not hurrying because they have no pressing engagements, they engage in conversation and entertaining patter,

"come on, tell us what you think" they say to me, since I've just been sitting back and listening, from time to time joining in the laughter at some humorous comment,

"what I say," I begin, once the plates have been cleared away and replaced by coffee and dessert,

"is that we are only missing one thing: a fair and equal distribution of wealth, that's all," after this they continue conversing among themselves as the boat speeds along, a few leave the table, perhaps to get a bit of fresh air, of course I have also provided entertainment to help pass the time, a television array with a number of channels projecting on several screens mounted beside each other ready to show live coverage of a number of different places and events, all the passengers have gathered in front of the television screens and at the touch of a dial the event is under way, some of those who had earlier jumped from the boat have now come home again, while others remain in the city, recordings from the past as well as things happening now are appearing on the screens, the crowd is getting a bit boisterous, look, a number of scenes are showing at the same time: in a village a person is surrounded by a milling crowd, in a rice paddy a person is surrounded by a milling crowd, in a workshop a person is surrounded by a milling crowd, in a city a person standing beside a fountain is surrounded by a milling crowd,

"who are you!" they are asking

"Adam Enlightened" comes the answer

"what do you want" they ask again

"To utter the divine word" is the response

"are you a prophet?"

"no"

"are you a divinity?"

"no"

"what then?"

"I am neither prophet nor divinity, I am only Allah come to earth"

"what the hell. . ."

then all the television screens show the confusion, then a mango tree appears, thick with fruit whose sweet ripeness makes the mouth water, this is clear because the televisions are color, people struggle to get their hands on the fruit, the TV viewers respond to this with shouting and commotion, jumping to their feet, but then the commotion slowly subsides, they take their seats again, silent, all silent, the susurration of their breathing can be heard, then a low echo, massive and heavy, hovering in the air, "I am Adam Enlightened" they breathe out from the depths of their voices, like singing, then the singing becomes a growling and a roar,

Adam Enlightened understands without studying,

Adam Enlightened is drunk without drinking

Adam Enlightened sleeps with eyes open,

Adam Enlightened is majestic without a crown,

Adam Enlightened speeds along without paddling,

the boat speeds along, passing through boulevards, past tall buildings, unfinished buildings, neighborhoods, government offices, hotels, places of amusement, banks, stores, supermarkets, theaters,

Adam Enlightened beloved of the river's water, checks its flow with a small dam that provides continuous irrigation, even in the dry season,

Adam Enlightened is a power generation plant, the thunder of lighting, an orderly confusion of to-ing and fro-ing,

Adam Enlightened is a gang of construction workers, laborers patching leaking city water mains, ditch diggers laying cable, road workers surfacing roads,

Adam Enlightened is a long line for buying rice, a line of pensioners queued for benefits, a weekly wage line,

Adam Enlightened is a band of homeless, unemployed,

dangerous customers, hungry mouths,

the boat speeds on, shops explode, who is beloved of the Lord? warm dew, unblossoming blossoms, Adam Enlightened, on a street corner, shop corner, in the corners of happiness,

the boat speeds on, supermarkets explode

who is beloved of the Lord? an unbalmy breeze, smooth gravel, Adam Enlightened, raw ditch water, a government seat

the boat speeds on, banks explode, who is beloved of the Lord? unrustling branches of leafy trees, squirrels that don't hop and fidget, Adam Enlightened, fat sacks of grain in the storehouse, fatsos at table, fatsos unable to hop and fidget, the boat speeds on, hotels explode, factories explode, offices explode, places of amusement explode, villages explode.

TRANSLATED BY TIM BEHREND

HANNA RAMBE

The Longan Tree

AS SANTOSO SPOKE TO HIS MOTHER he started straight ahead, "It's not that we don't sympathize with you, Mother. We know how sad you must be at being forced to move. You were born in this area; we know that. But it's not just you who's affected — everyone in the village is.

"Whenever big money comes into an area, people have to leave, and it doesn't matter whether they're forced to give up a piece of heritage going back hundreds of years. The bottom line is, if you want to be modern, the traditional has to make way for hotels, factories, airports, multi-level highways, shops, dams and all the rest."

The upland breeze was brisk and had a chilly edge. Leaves were starting to fall. Several yellow leaves landed on the table. One dropped into Toso's cup.

"You see, Mother, even this here longan tree shares our concern. It's dropped a leaf in my cup as a sign."

The two looked up at the beautiful tree. It had stopped flowering and was now covered in tiny fruit.

It had been a long time since Ndoro Den Ayu, the matriarch, Toso's mother, had enjoyed the atmosphere of warmth and tranquillity that she was feeling this evening. How often could she? Her rambling house, inherited by her husband from his father, was virtually empty. Her six children had all left the nest.

Toso, who had come on his own to see her, had been living in Australia for six years and unless he was given a very lucrative job offer, it seemed unlikely that he would return. Further, his wife liked it in Australia, and their two children were now in school there.

Yayuk, her oldest daughter, lived in Jakarta. Her husband was a high-ranking government official and the two of them owned a house, land, a car, and all other material goods they might need. It was no wonder they had no interest in living in Yayuk's ancestral house, located so far away. For them, it was a nice vacation home. Apart from a cool climate, the area also offered numerous historical ruins.

Sri, the next girl, lived with her husband in Irian Jaya. They were both doctors attached to a religious organization. Their children went to a boarding school in Bandung run by the same organization.

Siti, her other daughter, was unmarried. She was a nun and lived in Larantuka. Since moving there she'd only been home twice, and then her main reason for coming back had not been to see her mother, but for official business.

Padmo, her second son, was a hotel operator in Bali. Only two things motivated him: success and money, and he changed wives as often as some people changed their clothes. His offspring were an unhappy lot, and Ndoro Den Ayu worried about the kind of upbringing her grandchildren in Bali were getting.

Adi, who was older than Toso, was the only one of her children who didn't have a degree of some sort. He was a slim, good-looking man who was very bright and popular. Nonetheless, he was not one for studying and had always preferred partying, singing and gambling to reading academic books. Over the years he had tried his hand at several businesses but with very mixed success. The company he now managed had a contract to develop a transmigration site on Seram, and he was now living there.

Ndoro Den Ayu's husband had enjoyed a successful career in the government and had inherited a considerable tract of land. Theirs was a prosperous and respected family and their way of life very European.

Ndoro Den Ayu had never imagined that in her twilight years she would be alone, not surrounded by children and friends. Most had achieved great success in their lives, and had outgrown village life. They were educated and sophisticated.

The family house had extensive grounds — if it were in Jakarta, a half dozen small houses could be built in the yard. And that was only the front yard visible to passersby. At the back of the house were pens for horses, cows and chickens and a rice barn, too. The house was located on a corner property adjacent to an vast area of paddy fields. The neighboring house to the left was another colonial style home now being used as the sub-district office.

One menial job that Ndoro Den Ayu liked to do herself was tending her dahlias. She planted dahlias around the entire edge of the open lawn. Her Dutch friends laughingly referred to her home as "Dahlia House." There were flowers in bloom the whole year round. She had dahlias of all sorts — from plate-sized to coin-sized, from single to crowned blooms, with colors ranging from white to vibrant red.

She derived true pleasure from planting and fertilizing the flowers, removing their withered leaves, and ridding them of pesky caterpillars. For years she, her husband, and their children had made it a habit to take their afternoon tea in the garden. Her late husband, who was also her cousin, never tired of praising her for her green thumb.

Ndoro Den Ayu knew no other life than the calm and tranquil one she lived. Thus, she found it difficult to comprehend why anyone would want to turn the area into a huge international tourist resort.

The high plain on which she lived had been a tourist destination since the early days and the longan fruit was the area's "trademark."

But the area was relatively far from the large cities of Java's north coast and, at one time, just getting there entailed a trip of a few day's time. It wasn't cheap either. It was understandable, therefore, that it had once been only the well-heeled Dutch people who had cars of their own who visited there.

But now the area was to be awash with tourists. Plans called for the construction of a large airport and a grand hotel complete with swimming pools, tennis courts, golf courses, souvenir shops, restaurants, an entertainment park, and all the rest. As luck would have it, the sub-district in which she lived happened to be the perfect place for such a resort. Once the decision was announced, the area's residents were asked to move with the provision, of course, that they would be compensated for the loss of their houses and land.

The powers-that-be announced that the resort would reap numerous dividends; there would be employment opportunities for both skilled and unskilled workers. The area's vegetable, fruit, and flower producers would have a ready market. Drivers of busses, horse carts, and taxis, as well as tour companies would have a sustained income from the steady stream of tourists. Wasn't all of this of greater benefit than preserving the languid, traditional life style of the place?

Ndoro Den Ayu, along with other older people in the area, had no real objection to the development plans. The only thing they objected to was having to move. She had planned to die here and to be buried alongside her husband on the picturesque mountain slope nearby.

Was there no other alternative for her but to move? She didn't need the millions of rupiah offered to her in compensation, because she knew she wouldn't live for too many more years. And her children and grandchildren didn't need the money either.

"Keep it for yourself," they told her, "and go abroad for a holiday." But she was tired of going abroad.

Unfortunately, as fate would have it, the airport was slated to be built right in the middle of her family's land, on top of her home and her longan trees. So she had no choice but to move.

"We haven't had time together like this for a long time?" she said to Toso, breaking the silence that had fallen between them.

"I know. The trouble is, we all live so far away. If you were to live with Yayuk, it would be much easier for us to get together."

"Last night, Tos, I made up my mind."

"And what did you decide?" His voice betrayed his anxiety.

"To do what you kids have asked — to move. I've decided to leave when you do. You'll be going by plane, won't you?"

"But where do you want to go? To Yayuk's or to Sri's?"

"First I'll go to Yayuk's. Then, if I get tired of that, I'll go to Sri's. After that, I'll visit you. I'll move from place to place."

"You wouldn't have to move around like that, you know. You could buy yourself a little land and a new house in Jakarta."

"What are you thinking? I'm seventy-three. The only plot of land I'm going to buy measures one by two meters. What would I do with a house?"

"Let's not talk about that size of plot right now, Mother. We've thought about this and made plans for a new home for you. We're worried about you and want you to be happy, even though we know it's not your choice to leave."

"And I thank you for everything you've done. But I'm not an orchid, you know, that can be pulled up and transplanted from one place to another."

"I know that, Mother. I found out that once you're in your thirties and have started to put down roots, it's very difficult to move. It was very hard for me when we first moved to Australia. For Naning even more so. But that's the way of the world now. People are transplanted."

"I appreciate your concern, Tos. I often think about people who have been forced to flee from country to country, refugees, like you see on television. From East Germany to West Germany. From Cambodia to Thailand. From Palestine to Lebanon. . . Compared with those people, we don't have it so bad."

"It's amazing how mobile people now are. But then getting around is much more easy than it used to be. Refugees can move to a new country and make a fresh start. Everyone, it seems, is on the move, as a refugee, a transmigrant, an emigrant, a guest worker or a tourist."

"Well, I'm not an emigrant, a guest worker, or a tourist. I guess that "refugee" would be the best term for me. It just seems such a shame that a family of our standing, with our acres of land and with so many gifted children should be turned into refugees. I'm too old to be a refugee. Even in the old days, when this area served as a guerrilla base, we never ran away. It's ironic, isn't it?"

"You have to do what seems right at the time, Mother. That's the only way to survive. Swimming against the tide never works."

"Toso! Since when did you start to compromise? Thank goodness your father isn't here to witness that. There was nothing your father disliked more than compromise."

"But these days, Mother, confrontation isn't always wise. It is possible to adhere to one's principles without being confrontational. I don't think there's any harm in appearing to compromise."

"Well that's up to you; you're a grown man now. But that's not the way you were brought up. . . It's getting a bit chilly, don't you think?"

"Yes, it is," Toso replied. "The sun's gone behind the clouds and the temperature has dropped."

"But these are to be our last hours here. I want to stay outside with you till the sun goes down."

Toso clapped his hands and a middle-aged woman appeared.

"Mbok, could you bring a warm jacket for Mother?"

"Yes, sir."

"And one for me, too, the one on the chair in my room."

"Yes, sir."

The servant soon returned with the jackets, and they put them on. Toso rose from his chair.

"Where are you going?" his mother asked.

"Out to the garden. I want to take a close look at the longan trees before they're ripped up to make way for the airport."

"I'll come with you. I'd like to say good-bye to those trees. They've had a long life history of their own."

"Can you walk that far? Won't you be too cold?"

"Not for this one last time. I think my legs can carry me."

Ndoro Den Ayu held on to her son's hand as they walked around the house, cutting cross the spacious lawn, towards the back. A few minutes later they arrived at the longan tree that stood closest to the paddy fields off to the right of the house.

Toso stared up at the tree. "If Grandfather planted this tree when he first moved into the house, it must be more than a hundred years old."

"It's trunk is certainly the biggest. Three men with their arms outstretched still couldn't fit around it."

"This one always had the most fruit. Didn't you tell me you once got one hundred and twenty kilos from it?"

"Yes, it was during a long drought, around the time the Dutch recognized our independence. Now what year would that have been. . .?"

"I don't know but it had to have been before 1950."

The two clicked their tongues in amazement and then moved on to the next tree, located about twenty meters away. This one was very full-leafed and though it's trunk wasn't as large as that of the first tree it was still a beautiful specimen.

"Your father planted this one before he went off to school in Holland. It used to have a lot of fruit too, but every once in a while it would fail. I remember a few times when it didn't bear any fruit at all."

"But I remember that Yayuk liked this tree the best because of all the birds' nests it had at the top. It was such a lovely sound they made."

"You still remember that, do you? And do you remember Yayuk trying to imitate the sound of the birds on the piano?"

They moved on slowly. It was getting colder; the sun had all but disappeared.

"And here is the queen of the longan trees on the Kusumo estate!" Toso said proudly of the next tree.

"That's the one I planted as a newlywed, just after I came to live in this house. That would make it the same age as my marriage."

For a few moments they stopped and lingered in awe. In fact there was nothing particularly special about the shape of the tree or the amount of fruit it bore. They were merely spellbound by the memories of the distant past the tree so easily brought back to life. As they stood beneath the tree they both seemed to be reaching out for something that had been proven to be intangible.

They walked on to the last longan tree. This was not aligned with the other trees but stood apart on the left side of the house. Dusk had fallen and only its silhouette was visible.

"Setiadi planted this one when he was commander of the guerrilla forces up here. I forget the exact date, but it must have been before the recognition of sovereignty."

"No, Mother. It was at the time of the Madiun Incident which would have made it September 1948. As Father told it, Setiadi wanted to leave behind a memento in case he was killed in trying to put down the uprising. He had no family after all."

"Oh, yes, that's right. But obviously he survived. It was after that he left the army to continue his education. And then he married Yayuk." Ndoro Putri Ayu turned to her son. "They might be only trees, but they certainly can evoke the memories."

"They certainly can," he replied. "Remember the garden parties you organized after the harvest. That would be a good draw for tourists, wouldn't it?"

"I suppose it would, but the trees are going to be flattened, aren't they? There aren't going to be any more harvest parties around here, with the trees decorated and with dancing, eating, and drinking."

"It's such a shame. But what I remember most isn't the parties, but carrying gift baskets of longan fruit to the head of the market, the head of the clinic, the chief of police, government officials and all the rest. I remember how glad they were to receive them and how they treated me with such respect, like Santa Claus. I couldn't believe it. They were just longan after all."

The two went back into the house to ready themselves for dinner. Dinner in the Kusumo household had always been a special occasion where formal wear was compulsory. The menu was usually European.

Toso came to the table wearing a jacket, all the better to ward off the cold. His mother appeared in a long black skirt, a cream-colored blouse, and a black waistcoat. Her hair was done up in a bun.

"What's with the black, Mother? Are you in mourning?"

"Black is supposed to be very fashionable, but I've never been one for fashion. Fact is, I am in mourning — for the land I have to leave behind."

Toso smiled but said nothing. He in fact ached inside but he didn't want his mother to see that he, too, was mourning for their land, soon to be ripped up to build an airport. Given his mother's age, her grief might be short-lived. But what about him and Naning, and their children? They would no longer have any roots. In the future, when they came to visit the family graveyard, they would probably have to come by plane, stay in a hotel and hire a tour guide just to find the cemetery. He prayed that the family plot wouldn't disappear along with everything else.

Following their meal they sat down to watch television but nothing of interest was showing. They began to talk about plans for moving.

"I'm not going to go to any trouble," Toso's mother insisted, "I'll just take a small suitcase with a few good dresses, my lingerie, and the family photographs. That's it."

"Nothing else? Not even the antique table and chairs, or grandfather's paintings, or the lamps from the palace?"

"What's the point? None of you kids or the grandchildren have any interest in them. Some people call them antiques, but they're really just imitations of European antiques. There's nothing special about them. I'll sell them. Setiadi can take care of that."

"Isn't there anything from Father's library that you want to keep? What about that international architectural certificate or the medal he got for his help in the revolution?"

"You're right. I will keep that certificate. The grandchildren in Bali or Australia can have it. It did spare our family from the Allies' wrath. But then, thank goodness we had longans too."

"I'm not sure if I remember that story, Mother."

"How could you forget it? It was after the longan harvest that year. . . Your father picked three sacks of longans and put them in the library, intending to give them to the guerrillas who were coming that evening to collect some guns and ammunition. I don't know how but it seems that the Allied Forces, who had come here on the tail of Japan's defeat, somehow got wind of the fact that your father was part of the underground.

"Anyway, they came and started going through the house, including the library. I was so nervous, I kept having to go to the toilet. If they found the guns your father could have been killed. During the search the architectural certificate fell out of a book.

The Allied Forces commander studied it closely and then began to ask your father questions. As it turned out, the commander was a member of the same organization in his home country of Australia. The man's attitude changed completely and soon he and your father were chatting away like old friends. When he was going to leave your father told him to take the sacks of longans to the base. The foreign soldiers were very pleased; they said they had never tasted such sweet fruit. But I tell you, when they were gone we all breathed a huge sigh of relief. Just think, if the commander hadn't seen that certificate, he would have ordered a much more thorough search and probably would have found the weapons which were hidden under a pile of charcoal in the kitchen."

"And did the guerrillas come?"

"Yes, they did. That night. Luckily it rained heavily all that night. Along with the weapons your father had hidden he also sent a note to the guerrillas, apologizing for not being able to give them some longan fruit. He told them that he had been forced to turn over the fruit to the Allies during a raid, that he had done it for their own safety. All of that for a dozen rifles, a few boxes of bullets and some medicine."

"That's quite a story."

"Had you never heard it or did you just forget?"

"I don't remember hearing it, Mother. I do remember you telling us that the guerrillas eagerly awaited the harvest season because of the high sugar content of longan fruit. And that when other food was scarce, longan fruit provided a good source of energy."

Suddenly it struck Toso's mother that their longan trees and all the joys and sorrows associated with them would soon be nothing but memories.

Toso, too, paused in thought. He was distressed by the fact that they would soon have to leave the area. What he found most depressing was his powerlessness to do anything about it. What made the situation more difficult was he couldn't talk about his feelings to the other people in the village. It was his duty to convince the local residents, his mother included, that such upheavals were run-of-the-mill occurrences, as were evictions and emigration. He had been given the mission to persuade his mother to move, to convince her that it was futile to resist.

Toso had succeeded in his mission; his mother had agreed to move, but inside himself Toso felt guilty and remorseful. If only he could change the decision, he thought. If only there was some way he could prevent the demolition of the family house, the family land, and its colorful past.

His mother raised her voice to say that the next morning she would have her breakfast under the longan tree, just as she always had. But this time for the last time.

"Will you join me?" she asked Toso.

"Yes, Mother. Wake me when you get up."

"All right."

AFTER RISING THE NEXT MORNING Ndoro Den Ayu knocked on Toso's door but received no answer. Worried that the sky might turn overcast, she gave up trying to wake Toso and hurried out to the garden. There, beneath the longan tree, she drank a cup of coffee and ate two fried bananas.

Twice the servants knocked on Toso's door, but found no response. Finally his mother began to grow anxious and decided to force the door open. Toso was lying peacefully in his bed, covered with a woolen blanket and an old knitted jacket of his mother's that he had found in the armoire.

He appeared to be fast asleep. It wasn't until they felt for the pulse in his wrist that they realized he was not going to wake up.

The house was in turmoil. How could Toso be dead? Ndoro Den Ayu, usually so formal in demeanor, was inconsolable.

"Here he came to persuade me to move when the fact is he himself didn't want to leave the ancestral home," she remarked.

The doctor who came to the house soon after determined that Toso had died of a heart attack. He was only just forty.

Ndoro Den Ayu maintained that behind Toso's death was the suppression of his sadness about the loss of the family house and all it symbolized, and his frustration at not being able to do anything to prevent it from happening.

When Toso was buried the old woman said her final good-bye: "All humans are powerless, Tos, even in determining their own lives. All we can do is follow orders. There will always be something more powerful than ourselves."

TRANSLATED BY PAMELA ALLEN

PUTU WIJAYA

If He Could Choose Again

WHEN OKI FIRST WOKE there was a bomb next to him. Thinking that it was just a part of his dream, he didn't pay it much attention. He put his arm around it and, hugging it like a pillow, slept for a few hours more. When he woke again, later in the morning, he nearly bumped his head on the bomb.

Now Oki was perplexed. He had never touched a bomb before. In films he had watched bombs were never that important — it was only their consequences that mattered. Now he was forced to realize that a bomb was not the simple thing a cameraman or film director made it seem to be. No, a bomb was something real, something hard and cold and loaded with complications, including the question of how to deal with it.

Oki was alone in the bed. His wife had left early for the market, and since it was now nine o'clock the children would be in school. This meant that he would have to deal with the bomb by himself. Asking help from the maid was out of the question. Iyem could wash and cook and break the dishes regularly, but, clearly, she was not the person for him to speak with about a bomb.

The bomb was like a baby crying for attention. But that, Oki knew, could be very dangerous, for at just a touch the bomb might blow up and destroy his body, his mind, and his emotions. A bomb could turn a person into a murderer. Oki only dared to look at it; he couldn't even leave it, because he was afraid that something might happen when he wasn't watching. In fact, when Iyem knocked on the door, Oki snapped at her to stay far away and locked the door.

Oki was now sure that the bomb was working, and the loud ticking that he heard made him suspect that it was a time bomb. If he was right, the bomb would explode all by itself. All Oki could do was to decide where to let it explode so that it wouldn't endanger too many people.

At that moment he suddenly thought of the people he disliked: a certain neighbor, the employer who had once slighted him, former girlfriends, and dishonest officials who had somehow gone on to become respected leaders. He also thought of the shacks of the slum dwellers who might be better off dead than living more miserably than animals. It would be easy for him to take the bomb and let it explode there. The only question was whether he would be considered a hero or a villain.

But Oki was not the he-man type, and he had no interest in becoming either a headline-grabbing hero or a criminal. It was easier for him just to keep on staring at the bomb. He thought of leaving the house and telling his neighbors to stay far away, but then he began to worry that this might bring him nothing but trouble. If he turned out to be wrong, he would be the butt of jokes for months.

For an hour Oki wasn't able to decide anything at all, but during that time his fear grew and grew until he could no longer bear to think about the problem. A choice had to be made. Finally, he took the bomb, and put it inside his shirt. He would carry it outside and deposit it some place where it would not harm anyone. But where? The houses in his neighborhood were packed closely together. There were people everywhere, especially since a market and a busy road were located nearby.

Dressed in a rumpled sarong and rubber sandals, Oki stood perplexed in front of his house. He knew he had to decide quickly what to sacrifice. There could not be much time left — maybe only another critical quarter of an hour. After that the bomb might explode at any time.

To avoid attracting attention, he clasped the bomb even more tightly against his body. What was he to sacrifice? His home? The house of a neighbor whom everyone disliked for being such a trouble-maker? The car of a foreigner who happened to be going by? The police station? An empty field?

Oki's confusion made his heart beat even faster. He was so tense he couldn't think clearly. But then, catching sight of a flagpole, Oki suddenly broke into a run. At the top of the pole, the tallest flagpole in the area, the Red and White fluttered gracefully. Oki climbed right up.

Just as he had hoped, he did not attract much attention, at least at first. But as he climbed people began to gather around the base of the pole — initially only people from the houses nearby, but by the time he neared the top of the flagpole, people had begun to stream in from across the road as well.

At first the people laughed at the sight of a man on top of the pole, but when they discovered the man was Oki, their neighbor, their glee became surprise. Ordinarily, Oki was reasonable and patient, a nice person. He was a straightforward person who would never do anything without good reason. If he were climbing a flagpole dressed in a sarong, there must be something extraordinary going on. They stopped laughing and rushed closer to learn what was going on.

A child broke off from the crowd and ran to the school to tell Oki's children about their father. The children reported the news to their teachers who advised them to go and find their father. One of Oki's children went home, but found the house empty because Iyem had gone to the flagpole with the other people. Meanwhile, Oki's wife, who had been shopping, drifted towards the site with the crowd.

"Come down, Oki!" everyone shouted, while looking up at the top of the pole.

Oki signaled for people to keep their distance. He pointed at his chest and the bomb hidden inside his shirt, but the people didn't understand. More and more people gathered.

"Oki! Get down from there!" Oki's wife screamed when catching sight of her husband.

Oki's children, who were standing next to their mother, joined in: "Come down, Father! Come down!"

Oki tightened his hold. The flag fluttered. He took the bomb and wrapped it in the flag. He looked down anxiously. There were so many people down there. It no longer mattered that among them were his neighbors, his wife and his children. He saw only that there were many people, and his desperation grew.

"Don't kill the baby!" his wife screamed.

"Baby? What baby?" someone asked.

Oki's wife wailed and pointed towards the bundle in Oki's arms. The crowd understood at once and their attention moved from Oki to the bundle. The crowd fell silent as they looked up anxiously. They no longer dared to shout, because they were afraid that Oki would drop his child if he were startled.

"Don't kill the baby, Oki! He's your child, too!"

Oki's children screamed along, their mouths opened wide: "Don't, Father! Don't!"

Most of the crowd dared not say anything. This was a personal problem, it seemed. And so they stood, doing nothing, waiting to give their sympathy to whichever side turned out to be right.

Meanwhile, at the top of the flagpole, Oki grew more and more afraid. He couldn't hear anything anymore — only the ticking of the bomb, growing louder and louder, thundering inside his chest.

"Go away! Go away, all of you!" he shouted at the crowd, trying to make them fall back.

But more people streamed to the flagpole and Oki grew more terrified. He started to shake, and the flagpole began to sway, passing on his fear to the people below.

Because he felt responsible for the situation he clutched the bomb more tightly. "Let me be the one who dies if it explodes," he moaned in despair.

He tightened his hold on the bomb.

"Don't do it!" his wife shouted.

"Don't, Oki!" the crowd's screamed. "Take pity on your child!"

But Oki couldn't hear. All he could do was hold the bundle tightly.

His wife kept on screaming. His children were crying, too. The crowd grew bewildered. The situation was tense and uncertain. Only one person, an officer-of-the-law, remained calm. He saw that the situation was growing critical, in urgent need of action, and that a decision had to be made, fast.

The man tugged at the arm of Oki's wife.

"So, does your husband want to kill your child?" he asked.

"Yes, sir!"

"Which of the two do you love more?"

"Both of them!"

"You can't! You have to choose one."

"I can't. I love both of them!"

The man shook his head, coldly. "The situation is critical. You have to choose: your husband or your child?"

But Oki's wife could not decide. She wanted both of them, and didn't want to choose. She preferred to cry and stare up at the top at the flagpole while waving her hand: "Okiii!"

Oki's children, who had been calling to their father, fainted from screaming too hard. This led the officer to act. When he saw Oki clutch the bundle tightly, he raised his rifle.

Oki's wife screamed. She threw her arms around his legs and began to scratch at him: "Don't, officer! Don't"

The officer was not to be distracted. He ordered the crowd to help. Then tens or hundreds, if not thousands, of hands rose up, their fingers outstretched, ready to catch what was to fall.

From up above, the sea of hands looked like a flat, soft, white surface. Oki didn't understand why so many hands were raised, as if ready to catch something. But when he saw the rifle pointing up at his head, he held on even more tightly.

Bang! A bullet struck Oki, but did not make him to fall. He clung fast to the flagpole.

Bang! A second bullet weakened Oki's hold.

Bang! Oki remained wrapped around the flagpole, but the bomb slipped from his grasp.

Wrapped in the flag, the bomb floated downward towards the tens, or thousands, if not millions, of outstretched hands that were ready to catch the falling object.

Oki was still concious enough to hear the fatal explosion. He saw in his mind the hands that were torn from the bodies of their owners and thrown into the air in a spray of blood. He saw hundreds, thousands, or millions of people lose their hands: those of his children, his wife, his neighbors, of so many people, all of them thrown right up in his face.

He groaned.

If he could choose again he would not touch the bomb. He would leave it lying there on the bed, as a disaster or a nightmare. He didn't know where it had come from or who had placed it there. More importantly, he would feel no sense of obligation and would cherish no hope of saving people's lives.

Tortured by the consequences of his actions, Oki slowly died. Even today his body still hangs there on that flagpole, like a piece of dried meat.

TRANSLATED BY MILDRED E. WAGEMANN

RATNA INDRASWARI IBRAHIM

Oh, What a Beautiful Woman

NIKITA BOARDED THE TRAIN. The men in the car stared. So, she was still the beautiful Nikita — even though she was now twenty-seven and the mother of two? She stole a glance; the eyes of several men clung to her. What a relief to know that she was looking good, though she had dressed herself rather hurriedly that day. But it was true, she was not wrong; she was as beautiful as ever. She had been in a film once. A minor role, perhaps, but the wide screen had shown her beauty and talent to their best advantage. Even the director had sung her praises as a rising star.

But what had she then gone and done? Fallen in love with *him* and gotten married! She had thrown away her years and wasted her opportunities. And now what was she but a housewife living in the depressing home of her in-laws where her beauty and very being were all but ignored.

Nikita felt a twinge. She had sacrificed so much to be a wife, a model wife, but what did *he* have the nerve to suggest that morning: "You know, Nik, the children are old enough to take care of themselves. Why don't you open a lunch counter at the front of the house? There are plenty of college students living around here and attending classes at the new campus. It would give you something to do and help to bring in some extra money, too."

She could hardly breathe just thinking about her husband's words. Didn't she have dreams, too? She had so many of them just waiting to come true. So shouldn't he, as her husband, help her to make them come true? Instead, he was telling her to open a lunch counter.

A few of the men in the car continued to stare at her until, finally, the heavy-set woman seated beside Nikita, spoke up: "When you're pretty, the men are always after you. But be careful, dear. It's when you marry one of them that you find out what men are really like. I noticed, you look upset. What, did you have a fight with your boy friend?"

Pleased by the woman's question, Nikita nodded her head. Nikita's husband didn't seem to realize that she was still a beautiful woman. Or was he intentionally trying to make her think that she had lost her looks? So that she wouldn't be tempted to exploit her self-potential? So that, to spare his ego, she would turn into a woman like the one seated next to her? At one time she might have been attractive too, but now she just looked old and worn out.

Even as Nikita cried inside, the eyes of the men in the car remained fixed on her. They danced and appeared to say, "Oh, what a beautiful woman!"

And it was true. No one could disagree. She was beautiful! If any man should say to others that she was no different from other women, that she had just an average-looking face, he was a man afraid of her beauty, one already ensnared, who would shamelessly blather compliments to catch her. Indeed a woman must be beware, for such a man will do anything to obtain his love.

But now who was it that was trapped? Her husband treated her like a servant now. Seeking distraction from the throbbing in her temples, she turned her attention to the woman beside her.

"You look down," the woman was saying. "Tell me what's wrong."

"I'm looking for a job," Nikita answered pointedly.

"For a beautiful woman like you, finding a job should be easy. Why not look for a rich husband instead? No man is going to ignore someone as pretty as you. It's a law of nature; everyone likes what's beautiful."

"You seem to know what you're talking about. Is it books or experience that's talking?"

"Experience is the best teacher," the woman quietly confirmed. "You might not believe it, but I used to be so beautiful that all the men in my village adored me. But I was young and stupid then and fell in love with a man who completely took over my life once we were married. All I can do now is regret my foolishness. I hope you don't end up like me. You're educated and single; you should have lots of opportunities. Just don't get married in a hurry — that is if you want to have a career."

Nikita felt like she had been kicked. She didn't want to end up like the woman beside her. And if she did, whose fault would it be? The problem with women is that they allow themselves to be tied down; it is they who let their husbands underrate them.

Well she for one did not want to be tied down or made to feel less than she was. She would make him aware that she was still beautiful and had potential. She would tell him straight out that it wouldn't be fitting for her to run a lunch counter. There were lots of other things that she could do. He simply couldn't go on ignoring her potential and her beauty.

NIKITA SPOKE TO HER HUSBAND about her experience on the train but all he did was laugh. "It's great having you for a wife. I like it that men are head over heels for you. Imagine that — you, the mother of two kids!"

Following that conversation Nikita took the train often to visit her mother, and while she found no small number of male admirers, when she told her husband about them, he paid no attention.

Nikita grew more restless. She tried to stifle the gnawing feeling inside her but her husband was of no help. He, with his college education, should take notice of her, and try to encourage her to show her true self. Maybe he wanted to make her his puppet that one day, when worn and used, he would toss into the waste basket.

No, she decided, she wasn't going to be anyone's puppet!

EVENTUALLY,WORN DOWN by her own thoughts, Nikita decided to follow her husband's suggestion and open a lunch counter in front of the house. She proved herself to be an exceptionally hard worker.

"You were just upset because you didn't have anything have anything to do," her husband told her. "The money's not too bad, is it? You've got a lot of students who are regular customers. Buy yourself some new clothes from the profits. Go ahead! I know that since we got married I haven't been able to buy you many clothes."

Regardless of his insensitivity to her dreams, Nikita decided she didn't want to lose her husband. And now that she had a job, she didn't want to give up her work either. She now had something to keep herself busy and was able to earn money with her own hands. Now she could afford to buy whatever clothes, make-up and accessories she wanted. Her work helped to muffle that gnawing sensation inside her.

After the work turned routine, however, Nikita found herself thinking about the heavy-set woman she had met on the train. She was a woman who had lost her beauty all because she had let her husband underrate her and because she herself hadn't bothered to keep up her looks or to show her true identity.

Well,she wasn't a handful of clay to be molded by her husband. More than anything else, Nikita knew that she didn't want to become an ugly woman who wasted her life away in the kitchen.

One day Nikita's husband had another suggestion to make: "We should give our bedroom to Mother and put the kids in her room. We can build an addition on the empty lot in the back. We, as the heads of this household, should sleep in the back anyway. That will keep good luck flowing through the house."

No more than a few days later a group of workers came to start building the addition.

NIKITA ALWAYS TRIED TO LOOK PRETTY for her customers. Her husband might not care if she maintained her former appearance, — a beautiful young woman with the potential for becoming a great movie star — but she did.

She took notice of the growing attention of her male customers; she saw them making eyes at her. That, however, was as far as she would let it go. No matter how bad things might be with her husband, she still felt close to him. In fact, the attention she found from her customers made her smile more freely. Unfortunately, it seemed that everyone except him noticed her charms — slender and tall (167 centimeters!), sensual eyes and lips and brown skin the color of freshly-dampened soil.

Nikita smiled. She still had time to discover the best things that life had to offer.

THE NEW BEDROOM WAS FINISHED. Nikita's husband seemed pleased when he asked her to take charge of decorating the room, but the moment she stepped inside the room, she began to feel hot.

"This room is so hot!" she complained. "We have to buy a fan!"

"Even if we do have extra money from the lunch counter, what do we need a fan for?" her husband queried. "If you're hot, open the windows. The extra money can go into the purchase of a gas stove. That way you can cook faster and it won't be so hard to wash the pots. I admit the room is warm but we're not getting younger and you don't want to get rheumatism from the cold."

Nikita said nothing more.

There was no way she could rest comfortably in the new room. The warm air seemed to cling to her, making it impossible for her to sleep in the afternoon or for her to get a full night's rest. She had to get up and start cooking at three AM, yet it was rare that she could fall asleep before one.

Following her husband's advice Nikita threw the windows wide open but the hot air that blew in made her even more uncomfortable. She was miserably hot; there was no way she could take a nap in such heat. Once, in restless desperation, she stripped herself of all her clothing. Within minutes she was dreaming that she was asleep in a cool forest. Thereafter, whenever Nikita wanted to take a nap she first took off all her clothes.

One day Nikita dreamt she was asleep in the forest when, all of a sudden, all the flowers started to bloom. It made her want to sing, but then she noticed one of her customers spying on her. She felt violated and began to scream when the young man attempted to get closer. In an instant she was awake. No one was around. Had it been just a dream?

The next day, when Nikita was napping, she again felt that she was being watched. The man watching her was the young boarder at the house next door. He spoke to her with his eyes: "You're beautiful, Nikita. Such a gorgeous woman you are."

"How rude! Don't talk to me like that," Nikita growled as she covered her body with a thick blanket, "What do you think I am!"

A few days later, Nikita's young admirer came to her lunch-counter to eat. She wanted to tell him not to spy on her, that it was a rude thing to do, and that she was not a cheap woman.

The young man seemed to know that Nikita was mad. He spoke with his eyes to her: "I adore you, Nikita, and think you are the most beautiful woman in the world. . .after my mother, that is."

This statement made Nikita's chest swell and conquered her

unease. The young man's thoughts made her feel like a goddess afloat in the refreshing waters of the open sea.

Thereafter, every afternoon, as if by agreement, Nikita would display for the young man her beauty. In turn, the young man would praise her to the heavens and both would be left feeling pleased. Nikita swore to herself that there was no sexual desire involved. This was something she did for joy. She found from the act a happiness difficult to describe, something that left her feeling both pleased and awed. It also gave her greater perspective on the limits a husband has as a lover.

Even after all this, Nikita still spoke formally to her customer when seeing him at the lunch counter. It created no problems with her husband either. If anything their feelings for each other had grown stronger. For that reason alone, Nikita felt no wrong in allowing the young man to admire the beauty of her body.

No, nothing had changed between Nikita and her husband. So every afternoon she found herself engaged in an act that stimulated a welter of emotions; when the young man stared at her she found herself both happy and sad.

Then, one day the young man came to say good-bye. He had graduated and was going to start work in another city. He took his leave just like any other customer would. Nikita said good-bye to him just as she would to any other customer and expressed the hope that he would some day find the time to visit again.

After the man had gone, Nikita closed tightly the window of her room. No matter how tired she was, she didn't take afternoon naps anymore.

Nikita's husband noticed the changes in her. "You haven't been looking right," he told her one day. "And your cooking doesn't taste good either. Do you want our customers to switch to that new place that just opened? I don't know what you're thinking, Nik. Ever since you opened the counter you've been able to buy as many clothes as you want and still save some money for the children's school. You have to start cooking good food again."

"Oh, I can cook delicious food again, but is that all I am to you — a good cook who brings in cash for the family? Don't you think I'm pretty, that maybe, with your support, I could be a movie star?"

"Why are you fishing for compliments? What is this talk about your beauty and being a star. We're not getting younger, Nik. The important thing now is that we save enough money to be able to put the kids through college. But for that to happen we must to work together. It's too much for one person to do alone. And don't you think that a woman is happier if she's independent and not forever relying on her husband? Let's not repeat history, Nik. It was you who told me that your parents couldn't afford to put you or the other kids through school because they hadn't worked hard enough or tried to put money aside. Do you want the same thing to happen to our kids? Of course you don't!"

That afternoon, and every afternoon thereafter Nikita took off all her clothes when she rested. Who cared if a few young men spied on her? Who cared what was in their eyes, whether it was lust, shyness, or awe?

Nikita didn't care about them, but because he failed to see her beauty, she had to find that recognition from others. Stripping herself naked was thus for her the wise thing to do. . . That way she needed no other man. She would always be loyal to him!

TRANSLATED BY LISA C. HO

SENO GUMIRA AJIDARMA

Maria

FOR ONE YEAR NOW MARIA has been waiting for Antonio but to this day he hasn't returned. For one year she has left the front gate, the door to the house, and the windows open, just a little while longer each evening, hoping that Antonio will appear in the distance, walking towards home, and then break into a run to embrace her. But no one has appeared at the gate. No one has run to hug her or called out "Mama!"

How very much she misses Antonio, her hard-headed but happy-go-lucky boy. Though he has proven to be just as stubborn as Ricardo, his older brother, who has been missing for a long time, too, with no word of his whereabouts.

Gregorio, her strong-hearted husband, is also gone. She heard that his body was cut into pieces and scattered around like scraps of offal. That was when she also lost Ricardo, her oldest, hot-headed, son, who swore to avenge his father's death. She heard that he had turned into an exceptionally cruel war machine. People say that he makes sure enemy soldiers die in incredible pain. He is now a butcher.

The loss of Gregorio broke her heart, Ricardo's departure extinguished her inner-flame; Antonio's disappearance left her confused. The only things Antonio knew how to do were play the guitar, sing, and dance. So handsome was her younger son with his long and wavy hair, his smooth voice, and gentle eyes. But in the end he, too, had begun to burn inside. She often told him how Gregorio's death had broken her heart, how much it grieved her to know that Ricardo was a bloodthirsty killer, and that he was now the only reason she had for living. But Antonio, oh, Antonio, he was only in his teens, yet he felt that he must teach his mother the meaning of freedom.

For one year, a whole year now, Maria has let herself believe that at any moment Antonio might appear on the horizon. She knows that's where she'll first see him, her younger boy, his hair golden in the light of the setting sun and tossed by the wind from the coast.

For one year, a whole year, Maria has let herself believe that, hope against hope, at any moment she will see Antonio standing there. She will embrace him, her young boy, so strong and handsome like his father, and walk with him to the beach, all yellow and blue, where he will tell her everything. And though it is his mother with whom he speaks, he will tell his tale in intermittent phrases, like a young man declaring his feelings to his love. Oh, how very much she misses him.

Maria yearns to remind Antonio of the sound of waves, the voice of the wind, the whisper of the leaves, as she used to do, singing of them to him when he was a baby and she and Gregorio took him to the beach while little Ricardo scampered in the waves.

"It's been a year, Maria. Enough. . ." her sister Evangelista advised, though she herself knew how difficult it was for Maria to free her mind of thoughts of Antonio.

One year ago Maria had said, "He's still alive. No one has found his body."

Of course his body has not been found, was Evangelista's thought. They took it away in a truck. "And when they loaded the bodies onto the trucks," someone had told her, "they didn't distinguish between the dead and the almost dead."

Had Antonio been one of the dead or the almost dead? There were so many people who had not returned.

"They haven't found him, Evangelista. He must have escaped to the countryside and joined Ricardo. He will return."

Poor Maria, Evangelista thought, but Maria wasn't the only one who had suffered losses. There was no family that had not suffered. All had victims or disappearances.

"I'm sure he's alive Evangelista. My Antonio will return."

NOW A YEAR HAD PASSED, an entire year since the incident. Maria didn't want to think about it. She didn't want to think about it ever again. So strong was her desire to consider that none of it had ever happened, it was impossible to think about it anymore. She wanted everything to be quiet and calm, as peaceful as it had been when Gregorio was alive. And Ricardo was still with her. And Antonio hadn't disappeared without a trace. At the very least, like it had been when Antonio was still there, before the incident one year ago.

"I've also lost my children, Maria, three of them. . ."

"I've lost my husband, Maria. . ."

"I've lost my whole family, Maria. . .

"I'm alone in the world, Maria, but you still have me: Evangelista."

For a year, one whole year Maria has prayed for Antonio to return. Every evening, as night falls, when she closes the gate, shuts the door, and latches the windows, she still believes there is reason to hope. She will fetch a cold glass of beer for her son, light of her life, lay out clean clothes for him, and ask him to tell her what happened. She won't ask him to speak of blood and tears. Tales of suffering no longer interest her, for they are all too very much a part of daily life. Oppression, animosity, and degradation are subjects Maria does not ever wish to discuss. They do nothing but stir up resistance, and it is resistance that, through the ages, has always been paid for with pain and lives. How very dear the price must be for them to walk with their heads held high. Maria didn't want to hear of it anymore.

For a year, one year now since the incident, Maria has sat watching the flickering light of dusk and feeling that at any moment Antonio will appear, just as he used to, before there was talk about sovereignty and ideals. She wanted to listen to Antonio speak, to have him tell her about anything at all, small talk about his girlfriends: Rosa, Conchita, and Sonia. Oh how the women flocked around her handsome Antonio.

YES, IT'S HAS BEEN A YEAR FOR MARIA, but only one year. There are other women, other Marias, who have waited much longer, many more years, holding open a little while longer each evening their gates, and doors, and windows. And many who have given up hope that someday their lost children will return, and have stopped opening their doors and never go out again.

Many women have buried themselves so deeply in sadness there isn't anyone or anything capable of reviving them — not the resistance, not the rebellion. There are Marias who open the door and wait and Marias who close the door and wait, not knowing when their children will return.

THE DOOR TO THE HOUSE WAS STILL OPEN. Maria could see outside soldiers in formation. For years they had passed by the house but it was not a sight she had ever gotten used to. It was a sight still foreign for her.

The sound of marching had just begun to fade in the distance when she heard the squeak of a gate. It was dark, already night. She had become so lost in her reverie she must have forgotten to lock the gate. She heard the sound of footsteps on gravel and then, all of a sudden, there was a man standing before her. The person knelt and embraced her.

"Mama! I'm home, Mama!"

Maria did not move. She sighed.

"Antonio?"

"Yes, Antonio, Mama, your Antonio! Don't you recognize me?"

Now seated on the floor before her was a young man, but Maria didn't know him. His scalp, so full of scars with uneven patches of hair, resembled a strip-logged forest. The man's left eye was sealed shut, and his right eye, though open, was squinted, half shut. His face was full of scars, diagonal cuts running downward from both right to left and left to right. He had no ears and his nose looked completely out of place, as if it had somehow been moved form it's original home. His lips protruded grossly and his front teeth were missing. His clothes were nothing but rags and he wore no shoes. He had no fingernails or toe nails; they must have been pulled out by force. He was rail thin. Only in his half closed eye did there appear to be a sign of life, an ember. The rest of the man was wreckage.

"You are not Antonio."

"I am Antonio! I'm your Antonio!"

The wreck of a man shook Maria.

"You're not Antonio," she told him. "My Antonio is handsome, an angel. No, you're not Antonio."

"They beat me Mama! They beat me everyday because I wouldn't confess! But I didn't do anything, Mama. I didn't have anything to confess anything but they still beat me! They destroyed my body, Mama! My friends would not recognize me. My mouth is so damaged my voice has changed, but I am Antonio! You must believe me!"

"You're not Antonio. You're some other Antonio."

Evangelista came in.

"Evangelista! Tell Mama that I'm Antonio, her son!"

"Who are you? Who is this?" Evangelista asked Maria.

"Evangelista! Don't you know me either! Look at me! I'm Antonio! They destroyed my body but they couldn't destroy my spirit! They beat me every day because I wouldn't confess, but it only made me stronger! I'm not the Antonio I once was, Evangelista, but I am still your nephew, Ricardo's brother, the child of Gregorio and Maria!"

Evangelista put her arms around Maria from behind. The two women looked at the man as if he were a creature from another planet.

Almost simultaneously they said, "You are not Antonio. Now leave!"

The man who claimed to be Antonio paused momentarily. The ember in his half shut eye flickered and grew dim. A dream of three hundred and sixty-five nights had vanished in the space of a second.

"It's been a year," he said. "For a year I have longed for this meeting." He took a deep breath. "Mother, Evangelista, I'll go, though I know no better place to return to than here. Maybe it isn't time for us to be happy. The world, it seems, is no longer our home. You might not recognize me, but believe me when I say there is no Antonio besides me who is part of your family. Good-bye. Take care of her, Evangelista, in the name of my love for her."

Maria and Evangelista sighed, then murmured as one, "You're not Antonio. Please leave."

The wreck of a man pulled himself together and walked away. The women listen to the sound of his footsteps on the gravel, the sound of the gate being closed, and the rising wind.

Maria stared, empty eyed. "Close the windows, Evangelista. That crazy man might try to come back."

"Don't worry, Maria, I'm here with you."

Evangelista closed all the windows. When drawing the curtains she stared outwards. There in the darkness she could see the man, rubbing his half-shut eye as he walked slowly away, dragging his feet, and disappearing further and further into the obscurity of night.

She could hear very faintly the sound of soldiers on the march.

TRANSLATED BY MEREDITH MILLER

TITIS BASINO

The Drafting Table

WHEN I FIRST MARRIED, we lived in a small house. Our house was so small that it took less than an hour to clean. There were only two rooms.

In the back was a garden where together we'd count the new plants as they sprung up. Our early life together was one of great closeness.

Beside the house was a garage. But as my husband had only just graduated from engineering school, we didn't have enough money for a car, not even a used one. So I made use of the space.

Each morning my husband left for his job at a government office. He, along with three co-workers, were picked up and dropped off by an office car each day.

Every morning I would wave to him as he left for work and then, reluctantly, would begin to tackle the housework. At first I felt inept at everything, especially cooking, and I would sit at the kitchen table, leafing through the cookbook and contemplating for long periods of time what to cook.

What would be the easiest thing to cook, I wondered, as I went through the book. Everything seemed so complicated. And the ingredients were all expensive, far too dear for the salary of a young engineer fresh out of school.

One day, unable to figure out what food to prepare that day, I went into our room. In the room was a table, my husband's drafting table. On the side of the table was a knob that, when turned, allowed the table to tilt up or down, to the right or left, and at a slant.

For a long time I stared at the drafting table, which doubled as our dining table.

My husband often sat in front of the table, contemplating for long stretches of time. But he thought about other things, no doubt, not about cooking as I was now doing.

On the table were a number of sketches. The drawings weren't clear and I had no idea what they were for, but at the top of one sheet were written the words "trial home" and, at the bottom of the page, "side view" and "front view."

I gave the sketches no more thought; I had to get back to the food I had yet to prepare.

I decided to work on the laundry first and later buy what I needed from one of the passing vegetable vendors.

As I was gathering the dirty laundry I heard the call of a vendor outside. This one turned out to be a small and comical-looking man.

With a number of shirts still in my arms, I stood before his cart inspecting the vegetable seller's produce. The man appeared to be able to guess what was on my mind.

"And what will it be for the young missus today?" he asked. "What are you going to cook? Stir-fried vegetables? Chicken soup? Or maybe chicken gizzards and greens?"

I felt my face flush. For one thing I didn't like my new title, "young missus," and, for another, I felt that he was mocking me. He might have been joking but I truly felt that he was indirectly making fun of my husband's limited income.

I tried to keep my voice calm: "Today I think I'll cook. . . vegetables!"

"But you cooked vegetables yesterday," he immediately answered. "Why not make a lamb curry?"

"Because we don't eat lamb curry," I told him. "It causes high blood pressure."

The little man laughed gleefully.

That afternoon I placed on the drafting table a bowl of spiced vegetables, fried eggs and some chili sauce. Truly a meal for newlyweds, one cheap and easy!

I was asleep when my husband came home but jumped up when he planted a kiss on my cheek. But then the misery set in: Dear God, the food on the table was covered with ants and I had forgotten to remove my husband's drawings.

My husband wasn't upset. We'd only been married a month at this point and there were never angry words between us.

HOW QUICKLY TIME PASSES. Soon five years had gone by but we remained, through good times and bad, the closest of companions.

There came a time when a large project my husband was working on came to completion. The project manger, with whom my husband worked, laid off all the architects and sent the five engineers back to their former jobs. But the desks they had once occupied were now taken. The university, it seems, wasn't the only place where competition for a seat was high. At my husband's office, too, there were not enough seats to go around.

My husband grew increasingly irritable. He seemed exhausted, completely disinterested with life. The situation worsened and reached a critical point. By now we had four children and it was very difficult to make ends meet.

In previous times I would sometimes ask my husband if I should find a job to increase the family's income. Now I knew there was no point in asking; I had to act if there was still to be smoke in our kitchen. Little mouths needed milk, bread and vitamins. Their developing minds required games and books. I somehow had to provide.

I took a job in a private firm and paid a baby-sitter to look after my youngest child. Meanwhile, my husband, the idealist, took on teaching jobs at just about every technical faculty in this stifling city.

Opposition to my working was voiced by family members on all sides. It was especially difficult for me to deal with my parents-in-laws who did not like seeing their grandchildren being looked after by a stranger. In the end, however, they were forced to acquiesce once they realized that we were simply trying to provide a better life for our family.

By this time the drafting table had been moved to the garage which had become an office where students came to see their professor. Thus, I was no longer serving our meals on the table. It was now being used for its intended purpose.

If ever, late at night, I wanted to find my husband, I always knew I could find him at the drafting table, absorbed in some kind of work. It was a pleasure for me to have a companion when I had to stay up late with my own work.

One night, after I had finished my work, I brought out a cup of coffee to him in the garage. I looked over his shoulder at what he was doing. "This looks interesting," I said, trying to visualize his plans. "Is someone really going to build this?"

"Yes," he told me, "a certain Haji Jamal."

"He must be wealthy."

"And this is going to be my commission," he stated proudly while holding up a drawing of a family home.

"That's for you, is it?"

"No, Rani, it's going to be my gift to you."

And so, during the months that followed, even as he executed building plans for his clients, he was building a house for us as well. I was forbidden to see the house while it was under construction — it was to be a surprise anniversary gift.

I continued working. On the last weekend of each month I would take the children to the mountains.

Because of a heavy back load of work at the end of the month, my husband usually wasn't able to join us until a day later.

I liked the weekends in the mountains. Naturally, I found sleeping in such a cool place refreshing. Unfortunately, for my husband, there was always something that prevented him from joining us. He was too busy and "it's not like we're newlyweds anymore," he'd often say.

One weekend the children decided they didn't want to go to the mountains, but would rather go to their grandmother's. So I took the four of them to Cipete and then came back home. As I was lounging around the house I suddenly got the urge to see our new home. I completely forgot my husband's request that I wait until our tenth wedding anniversary to see the house.

I took the car and set off towards the construction site which was located in Pejompongan, behind the church.

From the outside the house looked finished. In front was a low iron fence. The yard was fairly large with a foot-high hedge around it. I couldn't bear to wait another moment to see inside.

I parked the car at the side of the street and walked up to the house. I was surprised to see that my husband's car was in the garage. He must be inside, I thought. But I didn't go straight inside. I went around to the side to a detached extension that was separated from the main house by a decorative pool over which arched a small footbridge.

The detached wing had four rooms. On their teak doors were the names of our children: Nora, Raja, Rima and Preli. I smiled to myself.

I then went across the footbridge, beneath which water lilies were already growing, and came to the main part of the house.

In front of the terrace, at a slightly lower level, was a rose garden. The black marble floor of the back terrace glistened like water. On the verandah were six chairs; dining chairs, I presumed.

I went inside but found the house deserted. Where was my husband? His driver, Pak Di, was asleep in the car, his mouth wide open.

The living room floor was covered with wall-to-wall carpet. The carpet was wine-colored with soft thick pile. Gray velvet curtains covered the windows and a glass wall. In the room was another set of six chairs. These were large and soft and white as snow.

I ran my hand across the back of one of the chairs. The, suddenly, as if doused with cold water, I jumped. I heard the sound of someone humming in one of the rooms. My husband never sang. I wondered who it could be.

I entered the room below the stairs. It was the master bedroom, our bedroom.

As the house hadn't been wired for electricity I was barely able to see. I looked around, waiting for my eye to adjust to the dark. One wall of the room was mirror-covered; on the facing wall was wooden cabinets. In the middle of the room was a white bed. And there, on the bed, was my husband, stretched out naked beneath a blue blanket.

Just as I was about to go up to wake him, the bathroom door opened and a slender body emerged, without a thread of clothing on. She stopped, startled, in front of the door.

The woman appeared to be as taken aback as I was. For a second I couldn't move, but then I began to seethe. As I fled the room I heard my husband calling out my name: "Rani, Rani!"

I ran to the car on the road. I could hardly put the key into the ignition for the tears that were stinging my eyes.

I'm surprised that I managed to get home. And there I began to cry. I sobbed endlessly and started throwing things, anything that I could get my hands on.

Finally, I plopped down on the floor, feeling completely weak and lifeless. I wanted nothing more than for the earth to open up in front of me and swallow me whole.

But then my husband was suddenly standing in front of me. From where I was seated, I stared upwards at his face. That face, which I had studied for almost ten years, was no longer mine. He had placed too low a value on himself.

I stood up, went towards him, scrutinizing his face and his mouth even as he began to apologize: "Forgive me, Rani, it was only the first time."

"Well that's great, Mr. Big Shot. For all I know you could have done it one-hundred thousand times, and still say you're innocent."

My hands shook as they tore open his shirt then ripped his undershirt. I beat my fists against his broad chest.

"Kill me, Rani. I'll let you."

"What? And have me jailed for murder? So that you can be finally free of me? Get out of here and take all of your things and your women too!"

I hurled a bottle of cologne at the medicine cabinet. As the mirror shattered, so did my heart. I ran into the bedroom and cried my weary self to sleep.

Thus marked the end of my marriage. Now my husbands spends his nights in night clubs surrounded by laughter and young women. I now live alone with my four children in our small but memory-filled house.

When it's cold at night I miss the warmth of a man's touch, a husband's. Sometimes the thought of remarrying flashes through my mind but then I remember that I am no merry widow. I am the mother of four children.

I pass the lonely nights with my pen in hand, writing for the various magazines that are scattered on the drafting table.

TRANSLATED BY CLAIRE SIVERSEN

Credits & Sources

ORIGINAL SHORT STORY CREDITS:

Fujinkai, Oh...Oh...Oh...! (*Och...Och...Och!*), **Surabaya**, **The Shorts** (*Kisah Sebuah Celana Pendek*), **From Kota to Harmoni** (*Kota-Harmoni*), **The New Java** (*Jawa Baru*), **Sanyo**, **Heiho**, and **Another Road to Rome (Jalan Lain ke Roma)**, from *Ave Maria dan Julun Lain ke Roma*, Balai Pustaka, Jakarta, 1975 (5th printing); **Why I Didn't Set up My Own Business** (*Mengapa Saya Ta' Jadi Dirikan Perusahaan Sendiri*), **A New Parliament in my Home** (*Parlemen Baru dibuka di Rumah Saya*) and **A Mayor's Downfall** (*Riwayat Jatuhnya Seorang Walikota*), from *Dengan Mata Terbuka*, Kuala Lumpur, Pustaka Antara, 1961; **His Balance Recovered** (*Mendapat Kepastian Jiwa*) from the author's files stored at the H.B. Jassin Documentation Center, Jakarta; **Paris, April 29** (*Paris, 29 April*), from *Kompas Minggu*, April 24, 1992, pg. 10; **Abus**, from Kompas, May 4, 1987; **Adam Enlightened** (*Adam Ma'rifat*), from *Adam Ma'rifat: Kumpulan Cerita Pendek.*, Balai Pustaka, Jakarta, pg. 16; **The Longan Tree** (*Pohon Lengkeng*), from *Horison*, Vol. XXVII (1992), No. 7, pg. 239; **If He Could Choose Again** (*Kalau Boleh Memilih Lagi*), from *Bom*, Balai Pustaka, Jakarta, 1992; **Oh, What a Beautiful Woman** (*Perempuan Itu Cantik*), from *Kado Istimewa: Cerpen Pilihan Kompas 1992, Harian Kompas*, Jakarta, pg. 51; **Maria**, from *Saksi Mata*, Yayasan Benteng Budaya, Yogyakarta, 1994; and **The Drafting Table** (*Meja Gambar*), from *Horison*, Vol. XI pg. 271 (1976).

TRANSLATION CREDITS:

The translation of **Fujinkai** that appears herein was first published in *Indonesia*, No. 2 (October 1966), pg. 125; **Oh...Oh...Oh...!** (*Och...och...och*) first appeared in *Perspective of Indonesia: An Atlantic Monthly Supplement*, June 1956, pg. 31; **Surabaya** (*Surabaja*) first appeared in *Indonesia*, No. 5 (April 1968), pg. 1; **The Shorts** (*Kisah sebuah Celana Pendek*) first appeared in *Eastern World*, Vol. V, No. 12 (Dec. 1951), pg. 30; **From Kota to Harmoni** (*Kota-Harmoni*) first appeared under the title "Kota Harmoni" in *Indonesia*, No. 45 (April 1988), pg. 105; **Why I Didn't Set up My Own Business** (*Mengapa Saya tak Jadi Dirikan Perusahaan Sendiri*) first appeared in *Indonesia*, No. 53 (April 1992), pg. 165; and **Another Road to Rome** (*Jalan Lain ke Roma*) first appeared in *Indonesia*, No. 34 (October 1982), pg. 41. These stories were reedited for the purposes of this publication and may not be reprinted without the permission of both the original copyright holder and The Lontar Foundation. All other short stories by Idrus were translated specifically for this volume, the English-language copyright for which is held by The Lontar Foundation.

ESSAYS:

Religious Restrictions (Menulis di Perbatasan), **Lessons in Scholarship** (*Iklim Akademik di Indonesia*), and **Political Prohibitions** (*Sensor dan Terbitan Politik*) are three working papers prepared by the authors for presentation at a seminar on the topic of freedom of expression that was sponsored by the Association of American Publishers in September 1996. Copyright to the Indonesian language version of these papers is held by their respective authors. Copyright for their English-language translation is held by the Lontar Foundation.

POETRY:

The poems "Lumbering Oxen (*Lembu yang berjalan*)," "From Regions of Question (*Dari daerah-daerah yang bertanya*)," "Asia Reads (*Asia membaca*)," "Myths of Regret (*Mitos-mitos kecemasan*)," "My Girl (*Gadis kita*)," "He Who Guards the Night (*Yang terjaga di malam hari*)," and "Our Inheritance (*Warisan kita*)" come from the collection *Those Living in Language* (*Yang Berdiam dalam Bahasa*) privately published by the author. All translations by John H. McGlynn.

Lontar Publications

The Lontar Foundation is a non-profit organization whose aims are fostering greater appreciation of Indonesian literature and culture, supporting the work of authors and translators of Indonesian literature, and improving the quality of publication and distribution of Indonesian literary works and translations. For more information about Lontar and its activities write to: Jl. Danau Maninjau No. 90, Pejompongan, Jakarta 10210. Or visit the foundation at its website (http://www.lontar.org).

Lontar's previous publications include the following:

Suddenly the Night
(ISBN No. 979-8083-00-8)
Suddenly the Night is an anthology of poetry by Sapardi Djoko Damono. As is stated in the introduction to the book, "More than any other contemporary Indonesian poet, Sapardi realizes that poetry is more than convention and that convention is not necessarily a requisite for poetry. Through the language of his poetry and its meaning, sound, and rhythm Sapardi proves himself capable of depicting a highly imaginative awareness of experience."

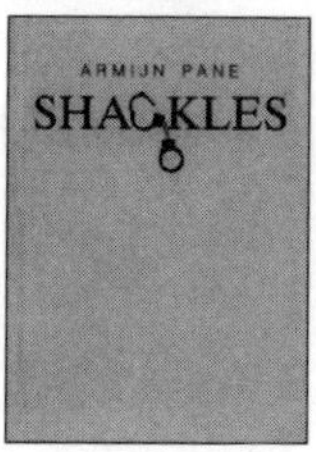

Shackles
(ISBN No. 979-8083-10-6)
Shackles, by Armijn Pane, is Indonesia's first psychological novel. Dr. Sukartono and his wife, Tini, find their marriage devoid of warmth and, in the midst of this turmoil Dr. Sukartono meets Rohayah, a woman who is ready to give him the security he lacks at home. The love triangle of *Shackles* illustrates the confusion felt by pre-independence Indonesians who had struggled to overcome the problems of a traditional society but who found that the shock of becoming a new type of person, one neither Eastern nor Western, was even more severe.

Walking Westward in the Morning
(ISBN No. 979-8083-03-2)
This book, reflecting the myriad mix of cultures that forms Indonesia, contains a collection of poems by seven of Indonesia's leading poets. What binds the writers and their poems together is the writers' willingness to deal with, not distance themselves from, problems affecting not only themselves, but also their nation and their fellow man.

On Foreign Shores:
American Images in Indonesian Poetry
(ISBN No. 979-8083-02-4)
On Foreign Shores is a poetic record of travels by Indonesian poets through the United States. For the writers who have spent time in the United States, the country that is America is sometimes a jungle, sometimes a labyrinth of loneliness, but at other times a snow-swept plain, a misty morning sky or a fount of pleasure and love. The poets paint a gamut of images that, while oftenfamiliar, take on a new light as they are seen through foreign eyes.

The Weaverbirds
(ISBN No. 979-8083-05-09)
This landmark novel by Y.B. Mangunwijaya is a tale of both physical and spiritual struggle. Larasati and Setadewa are childhood playmates, but as adults they find themselves on opposite sides of the political spectrum. The tactics that these two individuals adopt in dealing with the problems that beset their country offer guidance to survival in a chaotic world.

Golden Letters: Writing Traditions of Indonesia
(ISBN No. 979-8083-06-7).
This bilingual English-Indonesian catalogue offers a look at Indonesian manuscript treasures found in the manuscript collections of Great Britain. Lavishly illustrated, this book contains reproductions of letters and other written works in more than ten different scripts.

Shadows on the Silver Screen
(ISBN 979-8083-04-0)
This book by Salim Said is the first comprehensive history of the Indonesian cinema. Its publication begins to fill a major gap in Western film knowledge. Of all the arts, film is the most political: it is the most responsive to the political climate and the most tempting target for political manipulation. This book offers a critical look at the political and social forces which have shaped Indonesian film over the last sixty years.

Menagerie 1
(ISBN No. 979-8083-07-5)
This volume is the first of an occasional series focusing on the Indonesian short story but also including literary and pictorial essays and poetry.

Time Bomb and Cockroach Opera
(ISBN No. 979-8083-11-3)
Through street talk and raunchy humor the two plays in this volume present a stinging critique of social injustice. In a slum on the banks of a fetid canal, society's victims, the cockroaches of this world — the poor, prostitutes, beggars, and thieves — play out their struggle with life. They are the bomb ready to explode. *Time Bomb and Cockroach Opera*, showing the dark "underside" to elite prosperity, subvert rather than affirm common assumptions.

The Bottomless Well
(ISBN No. 979-8083-10-5)
The plays of Arifin C. Noer are an inexhaustible commentary on Indonesians and Indonesian society. *The Bottomless Well* is no exception, Since its first performance in 1964, *The Bottomless Well* has been one of Indonesia's most frequently produced plays.

Menagerie 2
(ISBN No. 979-8083-13-X)
As wide-ranging in theme as the first volume in Lontar's short story series, *Menagerie 2* offers readers a new and different tour of Indonesia through its literature.

Sidelines: Thought Pieces from Tempo Magazine
(ISBN No. 979-8083-21-0)
In *Sidelines*, Goenawan Mohamad, Indonesia's most prominent essayist, reveals an Indonesia which exists beyond the headlines. He writes about identity and change, democracy and freedom, and the meaning of history. This book gives an unrivaled insight into a complex country with a many-layered past.

Former Points of View: Postcards & Literary Passages from Pre-Independence Indonesia
(ISBN No. 979-8083-22-9)
Published in conjunction with the fiftieth anniversary of Indonesian independence, this beautifully illustrated book gives form to an era now gone forever. As with a family photograph album, this book offers readers an opportunity to leaf through pictures of sometimes familiar, sometimes forgotten faces and former points of view.

Early Views of Indonesia: Drawings from The British Library
(ISBN No. 0-7123-0431-2)
Published in cooperation with The British Library this book reflects, through the drawings it contains, the Indonesian island world at the time of the British interregnum, especially during periode when Thomas Stamford Raffles was Lieutenant Governor of Java (1811-16).

Illuminations: The Writing Traditions of Indonesia
(ISBN No. 0-8348-0349-6)
This book, containing fifteen chapters, written by nineteen of the world's foremost authorities and illustrated with over 380 full-color illustrations, offers the first comprehensive look at Indonesia's writing traditions. With its extensive visual documentation, this large-format book is both a visual delight and a valuable resource for the scholar, student, and artist. It is also a publishing milestone, recording many rare and precious manuscripts and preserving them for posterity.

Square Moon
(ISBN No. 979-8083-24-5)
In addition to *Square Moon* this volume contains translations of three other short plays by Indonesia's most well-known absurdist writer, Iwan Simatupang.

To Love, To Wander: The Poetry of Sitor Situmorang
(ISBN No. 979-8083-25-3).
The more than one hundred poems in this book trace the development of Indonesia's longest-reigning poet, from before the revolution through the turbulent 1960s and finally to his current residence abroad.